"As soon as he releases you, I'll take you home, but you aren't going to stay there."

Jackson continued, "We'll pack up a couple of bags for you and then you're coming to my place to stay while you heal."

"Jackson... I..."

"Please don't argue with me, Josie." He took her hand and squeezed it tight. "Somebody definitely tried to kill you last night and he didn't succeed, which means he'll come after you again. You need a bodyguard and I want that position. I'll make sure nobody hurts you again."

She stared into his eyes and tears filled hers. Was she going to reject his offer? He knew she was not only a strong woman, but a prideful one as well.

"Josie, please," he said softly. "If nothing else, do this for me."

MONSTER IN THE MARSH

New York Times Bestselling Author

CARLA CASSIDY

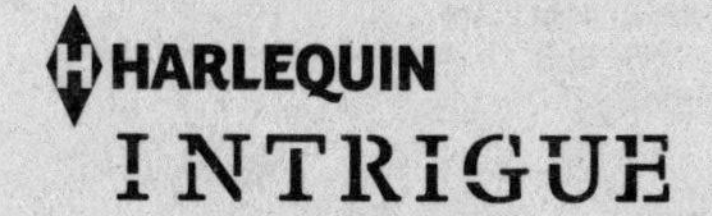

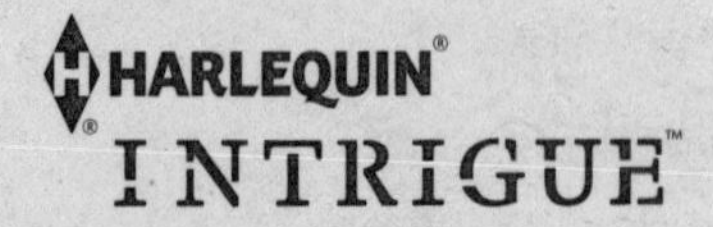

ISBN-13: 978-1-335-59139-5

Monster in the Marsh

For questions and comments about the quality of this book, please contact us at CustomerService@Harlequin.com.

Harlequin Enterprises ULC
22 Adelaide St. West, 41st Floor
Toronto, Ontario M5H 4E3, Canada
www.Harlequin.com

Printed in U.S.A.

Carla Cassidy is an award-winning, *New York Times* bestselling author who has written over 170 books, including 150 for Harlequin. She has won the Centennial Award from Romance Writers of America. Most recently she won the 2019 Write Touch Readers' Award for her Harlequin Intrigue title *Desperate Strangers*. Carla believes the only thing better than curling up with a good book is sitting down at the computer with a good story to write.

Books by Carla Cassidy

Harlequin Intrigue

The Swamp Slayings

Unsolved Bayou Murder
Monster in the Marsh

Kings of Coyote Creek

Closing in on the Cowboy
Revenge on the Ranch
Gunsmoke in the Grassland

Desperate Strangers
Desperate Intentions
Desperate Measures
Stalked in the Night
Stalker in the Shadows

Visit the Author Profile page at Harlequin.com.

CAST OF CHARACTERS

Josephine Cadieux—Lives in the swamp and is haunted and hunted by an assailant.

Jackson Fortier—A bored businessman. Does he have what it takes to protect the woman he loves?

Lee Townsend—Had his rage over his divorce driven him into the swamp to do the unthinkable?

Sonny Landrey—Had the single man ventured into the swamp for some sexual excitement?

Police Chief Thomas Gravois—How much does he know about Josie's assault and the murders of three women from the swamp? Whom might he be protecting?

Chapter One

Jackson Fortier pulled his car into one of the back parking spaces on the side of Vincent's Gas and Grocery Store. The little store was the last establishment before the vast swamp that more than half surrounded the small town of Black Bayou, Louisiana.

There were more than a dozen cars parked there as Vincent Smith, the owner of the place, allowed people who lived in the swamp to keep their vehicles there. His sleek sports car stuck out like a sore thumb amid the old model cars and banged-up pickups.

It was just after noon and the late August sun was bright and cast down waves of heat. He got out of the car and pulled a note from his pocket. On the sheet of paper were directions to his best friend, Peyton and her husband, Beau's shanty.

He'd never been to their place in the swamp before. Peyton had offered to meet him here and lead him in, but he'd insisted he was a big boy and with directions he could get himself there.

However, as he stood and stared up the trail before

him, he was sorry he hadn't taken Peyton up on her offer. Tangled vines, overhanging leaves and Spanish moss made the path disappear into semidarkness.

Where the sunlight did manage to penetrate through, it shone on pools of water on either side of the path, dark waters that were filled with gators and snakes and all sort of other mysterious creatures.

The only place Jackson was at home on a trail was when he was walking the greens on a golf course. He fingered the directions in his hand as a wave of apprehension shot through him. It wasn't too late to call Peyton and have her meet him here, but he was reluctant to do so.

Surely if Peyton could traverse these paths alone, then he could as well. He glanced down at the directions. *Go straight ahead until you reach a fork. Take the path to the left.* That's all he read. He'd look at the next part when he reached the fork.

He drew a deep breath and then began to walk slowly forward. There was a distinctive odor in the air. It was a combination of something sweetly floral coupled with greenery and earthiness and the distinctive scent of decay.

Insects buzzed and clicked all around his head, creating a cacophony of sound that was totally alien to him. A rustling came from either side of him as if small creatures were running away from his presence. At least he hoped like hell they were running away from him.

The apprehension inside him rose higher as he

forged ahead, watching every single step where he placed his feet. He admitted he'd been a fool to attempt this for the first time all alone.

He could easily fall into the dark waters on either side of the path and be eaten by a gator or bitten by a venomous snake and die an agonizing death. Hell, he could get lost in the vast depths of the swamp and never be seen or heard from again.

He'd like to think the sheen of moisture that covered his skin was from the heavy humidity that hung in the air, but he suspected it was the perspiration of fear.

Hell, he could face down a shark across the table in a boardroom and beat most any man in a financial game, but walking into the swamp had him on edge like nothing he'd ever experienced before in his life.

"Suck it up, man," he said aloud to himself. He crept along at a snail's pace and dodged the low hanging branches that threatened to take his head off. He jumped and cursed as a large splash sounded far too close for comfort in the waters to his left.

He took a couple more steps, then stopped and whirled around as a rustling noise came from behind him. His heart raced and his body filled with fight-or-flight adrenaline. He saw nothing. Hopefully, it was just another little animal scurrying through the brush and not a wild boar bent on eating him.

He turned back around and took another couple of steps. The rustling came again and this time when he turned around to look, his right foot stepped off the narrow path and directly into the dark water.

A string of curses escaped him as he quickly yanked his foot up and out. Dammit, it had been stupid for him to wear his good loafers and nice black slacks. All of his clothes, including the nice shirt he had on would probably be ruined by the end of this trek.

He stopped cursing and immediately heard the sound of musical laughter coming from someplace behind him. He whirled around again and there she was…one of the most beautiful women he had ever seen in his life.

She was clad in a pair of jeans and a white sleeveless blouse that showcased her deep tan. Long dark hair spilled down her back and her dark eyes sparked with obvious humor. "First time in the swamp, Mr. Fancy Pants?"

"What gave you that idea?" he asked with a touch of humor and a bit of embarrassment.

She laughed once again and even though he knew she was laughing at him, he couldn't take offense. He probably looked like a silly fool to anyone who had been watching him bumbling his way along. But he suddenly had other things on his mind besides his own embarrassment, like who was this beautiful woman?

"My name isn't fancy pants, but it is Jackson… Jackson Fortier. And you are?"

"Josephine Cadieux, but folks around here just call me Josie," she replied. "What are you doing out here in the swamp? It's obvious you aren't a frequent visitor."

"Definitely not. I'm on my way to visit with friends. Maybe you know them, Peyton LaCroix and Beau Boudreau?"

"I not only know them, I'm friendly with them," she replied.

"I agreed to come for a visit today and insisted Peyton didn't have to meet me to lead the way in and instead she could just give me the directions." He held out the piece of paper he'd been clutching in a death grip in his hand.

"They are close neighbors of mine. Would you like me to take you to their place?" she asked.

"That would be great," he replied with a sigh of relief. Not only would he like her to take him in, but it would also maybe give him a chance to get to know her a little better.

Her attractiveness definitely piqued his interest. And it had been a very long time since he'd been interested in any woman. He watched as she walked in front of him. "Just follow me," she said.

He couldn't help but notice the perfect roundness of her rear end, just as he had noticed the full breasts beneath her white blouse. The jeans she wore clung to her long shapely legs. Ah, there was no question that Josie Cadieux was a real stunner.

"Watch your step here," she said as the trail narrowed.

"Thanks. So, you mentioned you're a neighbor of Peyton's. Do you have a family?" he asked.

"No, it's just me," she replied. They reached the fork in the trail and she led him to the left.

"What do you do out here?" he asked. The fact that she'd said she lived alone had further intrigued him.

"I fish. That nice piece of red snapper or catfish you ate in one of your fancy restaurants in town might have been caught by me." She stopped and turned around to look at him. Her eyes held a teasing sparkle he found enchanting. "And what do you do besides wear inappropriate clothes for a visit to the swamp?"

He laughed, delighted that she had some sass to her. "I deal in real estate," he replied. It was an understatement because he dealt in all kinds of finance. It was how he'd become wealthy…and completely bored with his life.

She turned back around and continued forward. She moved with an agility and grace he admired. He followed after her, trying to step exactly where she stepped as he dodged Spanish moss and vines that threatened to consume anyone who got too close to them.

He tried to pay attention to where they were going but it was difficult to concentrate on anything but her. "So, are you single?" he asked.

"It depends on who asks me," she replied.

"What if I'm asking?"

"I'd have to think about it."

"How long would you have to think about it?" he asked.

"I'm not sure." They took a sharp fork in the trail and a shanty appeared. "That's Beau and Peyton's place." She turned and smiled. "You have arrived safely despite your fancy clothes and stumbling start."

"That's thanks to you," he replied. "You said you were neighbors of Beau and Peyton. So, where's your place?"

"Around," she replied, and there was something in her tone that let him know he'd overstepped boundaries with the question.

"So, are you usually around the same place around the same time where I met you today on other days?" He didn't want to leave here without some opportunity to see her again. He was drawn to her and wanted to get to know her better. She was so different from all the other women he had known.

It wasn't just that she was gorgeous, but it also had to do with her obvious self-reliance and the inner strength he sensed in her. He'd never thought much about the women who lived in the swamp, other than three of them who had been in the newspaper headlines recently as murder victims.

"I could possibly be around the same place again tomorrow," she replied. Once again, a flirtatious sparkle filled her eyes. "Are you sure you want to venture out here again?"

"Definitely," he replied. "Will you know tomorrow if you're single?"

She cast him a slightly mysterious smile. "We'll see tomorrow. Enjoy your visit," she said and took several steps away from him, quickly disappearing into the darkness of the swamp.

A DARK BAG stole Josie's breath away as it fell around her head to her neck and a string pulled it tight, threatening to suffocate her. Wha-what was happening? She raised her hands to get it off her, but a hard push cast her to the ground.

With a cry, she fell forward to her hands and knees. Before she could regain her footing or figure out what was happening, she was rolled over on her back.

Immediately, somebody was on top of her, grabbing her wrists and attempting to tie them together. She tried to fight back, but he managed to tie her wrists together anyway.

Shock and fear shot through her. Was this the person who had killed three women? Was she about to become the fourth victim of the Honey Island Swamp Monster?

Josie came awake and jerked up to a sitting position, her heart pounding a thousand beats a minute as sobs ripped from the very depths of her.

Looking around the bedroom with the aid of a shaft of moonlight that danced in through the nearby window, she tried to center herself. It had not only been a horrible nightmare, but it had been what had happened to her a little over ten months ago.

It took her several moments and then she managed

to stop crying. She swiped the last of her tears away and then slid her legs over the side of the bed and got up. She went into the living area and lit a couple of kerosene lanterns that were on a shelf. She could have started her generator and flipped on an electric light, but it was too much trouble and, in any case, she often preferred the softer glow of the lanterns.

There was no way she was ready to go back to sleep, not with the taste of the nightmare still bitter on her tongue and thick in her chest.

She went to her front door, unlocked it and then stepped outside on the narrow porch that encircled her shanty. The sounds of the swamp surrounded her…the throaty bellow of frogs and the slap of fish in the water. Insects buzzed and clicked in a nightly chorus and there was also the rustling of night creatures as they scampered along through the nearby brush.

She'd never been afraid in the swamp. It was her home. From a young age, her parents had taught her the good plants and the bad, the things to be afraid of and the places to avoid.

No, she'd never been afraid in the swamp until that night when she'd been violated and even then, it hadn't been anyone from the swamp.

The man who had raped her had been from town. His hands had been far too soft to be anyone from the swamp. He'd smelled of expensive cologne and even though he'd only spoken a few words to her, she knew she would never ever forget the sound of his deep voice.

She'd immediately reported the assault to the chief of police, Thomas Gravois. She knew if she'd been a young woman from town, Gravois would have moved heaven and earth to solve the crime. But because she was from the swamp, next to nothing had been done about it.

That didn't mean she was just going to forget about it. One way or another, she intended to find the man and expose him. However, there was a huge obstacle standing in her way.

As a woman from the swamp, she had no invite into the inner circle of wealthy men that ran the town of Black Bayou. And she believed with all her heart that was where her personal monster hid.

She thought about the man she had led in to Peyton and Beau's place. The minute she'd seen him, she'd known who he was. Jackson Fortier was one of the most eligible single men in the small town. He was not only wickedly handsome, but he was also extremely wealthy.

Josie didn't give a damn about his money, but he could potentially be an entry into where she wanted to go. Or she could possibly never see him again.

One thing was certain, he wasn't the man who had attacked her. She'd know the sound of her attacker's voice and Jackson wasn't him.

With the nightmare finally behind her and the lullaby of the swamp soothing her, she went back inside and returned to her bed. She stared up at her dark ceiling and finally sleep claimed her once again.

She awakened just after sunrise. She dressed quickly and went out her back door where a pirogue was tied up. The small boat was what she used to check the lines that she'd baited the night before.

She added her push pole and an oar, along with her tackle box and then she got into the pirogue and used the push pole to glide slowly away from her home.

Mornings in the swamp were positively magical as far as she was concerned. The sunlight dappled the glistening water with gold tones and birds sang from the treetops. Fish jumped high, as if rested by the night and now eager to show off their prowess.

There was a peace here, a reassurance that the ecosystem was working the way it should and all was well. She glided across the water, barely making a ripple as she used her paddle only when it was necessary.

Josie didn't need to make a lot of money. She paid no rent and had no utility bills. But she did need money for the gas she put in her generator to give her a little electricity when she wanted it. Just like any other twenty-seven-year-old, she liked to occasionally buy a new outfit for herself, although she had few places to go where anyone might admire her choice of fashion.

Most of the time, her money went into a large jug she kept in the closet in her bedroom. It had grown to be a healthy savings account, although she had no idea what she was saving it for.

Many of the women she knew were saving their money so they could, somehow, someday escape the swamp. Josie had never really had a desire to leave this place that was in her heart and very soul. There had just been two times when she'd wished things might have been different, but she didn't want to think about those times now.

She reached the place where her fishing lines were located and began to pull them up. She was eager to discover what had been caught overnight.

An hour later, she was heading home, pleased with her catch of the day. When she reached her shanty, she placed the fish she'd caught into a cage she had in the water. They would stay alive until she had enough caught to take them into town and sell.

Once the fish were squared away, she started her generator and went back into the house. Her parents had worked hard to make their shanty as updated as possible.

The generator not only provided electricity for lights and small appliances, but also a heated water system for showering. The only thing they hadn't been able to have was a working refrigerator. So, every couple of days, Josie went to Vincent's and bought ice and a few items to keep in a large ice chest.

Although she did much of her cooking on top of the potbelly stove, there were mornings when it was too warm, or she just didn't want to go to the trouble to build a fire.

She now plugged in a single burner cooktop and the toaster. She then got two eggs out of her cooler along with a stick of butter.

Minutes later, she sat at the small table in the kitchen area to eat. It was at this time when she missed her parents the most. The three of them had always eaten breakfast together. They'd talked about the day to come and share happy laughter. Unfortunately, her father had passed two years ago from cancer and her mother had followed him six months later and died from a massive heart attack.

The past year and a half had been lonely for Josie, although soon after her mother's passing, she'd thought she'd met the man of her dreams. Even though he'd been a town guy, she'd been certain their love story had been written in the stars. She'd been so wrong and that experience had taught her a valuable lesson.

She washed up her dishes and then went in for a quick shower. As she stood beneath the warm spray of water, she wondered if Jackson would really show up today. She intended to be there just in case he did, but she wouldn't be surprised if he didn't come.

After showering, she changed into a pair of capri jeans and a hot pink sleeveless blouse that she knew looked good on her. It always took her a few minutes to brush through her long hair. Normally, she didn't wear makeup, but today she put on a little mascara and then spritzed on her favorite perfume.

Just beneath the waistband of her jeans, she tucked in a sheath that carried a small but wickedly sharp knife. Since her assault, she never left the house without the weapon. She would never be caught utterly defenseless again.

By then it was time for her to leave. She grabbed her key to the front door, shoved it in a pocket and then left the shanty.

An edge of excitement raced through her as she headed back to the place where she had first seen Jackson the day before. A smile curved her lips as she remembered watching him bumble his way into the swamp.

Even though he'd been very tentative and she'd found him slightly comical, there was no question that he was a hot hunk.

His dark hair had looked thick and rich and his bright blue eyes had been unexpected yet beautiful. His facial features were strong and bold and wonderfully handsome. Even beneath his fancy lavender shirt, she could tell his shoulders were broad and his waist was slim. Oh, yeah, definitely a hunk.

If he did show up today, then it would mean he was interested in her. And if she played her cards right with him, then she might be welcomed into the wealthy inner circle and she'd potentially be able to identify her assailant.

If she didn't like Jackson, she'd pretend she did anyway. If she did like him then it would certainly make things easier for her. No matter what happened, she wouldn't lose sight of the reality that she intended only to use him for a little while to get what she wanted…what she needed, and that was justice.

She might pretend to have a romantic interest in him, but she wouldn't allow herself to catch any real feelings for him or any other man from town. That had been the lesson she'd learned after her past relationship. She'd been there, done that, and her heart would remain closed forever.

She finally reached the spot where she'd seen Jackson the day before. She was early. As she waited to see if he'd show up, a new rush of excitement filled her. She was putting herself out there as bait and all she was hoping for now was that Jackson would take the bait and run with it.

Chapter Two

Jackson had dressed more appropriately for his trek into the swamp today. He was clad in a plain light blue cotton shirt and a pair of jeans, along with an old pair of boots he used to wear to construction sites.

Would she be there today? God, he hoped so. The lovely Josie had been in his thoughts all night long. He'd asked Peyton and Beau about her. "She's an incredibly strong woman," Beau had said. "She was very close to her parents before they passed but she seems to be making her own way just fine."

"We don't know much else about her personal life," Peyton added. "She's always friendly, but she pretty much keeps to herself."

Thankfully, when he was finished visiting with Beau and Peyton, Peyton had then walked him out of the swamp and to his car. Now he was ready to go back in with hopes of meeting up with the lovely Josie again.

A sweet anticipation filled his veins as he parked his car in Vincent's parking lot. There was no question that if she didn't show up today, he'd be disappointed.

He stepped out of his car and into the noonday heat and humidity. He looked up the mouth of the pathway and into the thick foliage and murky waters.

There were many other trails into the swamp from all over the small town. What were the odds of meeting a beautiful woman on this particular path?

Even though it was still rather daunting for him to enter into the swampy interior, he wouldn't have to go far before he would be at the place where he'd first seen Josie.

He began the trek in, feeling a bit more confident than he had the day before. He still watched every step he took in an effort to stay on the narrow path.

He hadn't gone too far in when he saw her. She stepped out from behind a tree, a smile curving her lips. His heart beat just a little faster at the sight of her.

"You came," she said.

He grinned. "And so did you." He looked around. "Is there someplace we can go to sit and talk?"

"Definitely. Just come with me." She turned and started up the trail. He followed right behind her, wondering if she was taking him to her place. He was definitely interested to see the place she called home. He was interested in everything about her.

She turned on a path he hadn't been on before and then stopped abruptly. Ahead of her was a large downed dead tree trunk. She sat on it and then gestured for him to have a seat next to her.

Although he was surprised, he shouldn't have been. She certainly didn't know him well enough to take him to her house. "This is one of my favorite places to sit and think," she said.

He sat next to her, not so close as to intimidate her, but close enough he could smell the scent that emanated from her. It was wonderful, a combination of mysterious flowers and exotic spices that instantly called to something inside him.

She looked beautiful in the pink blouse that seemed to pull a little color into her cheeks and looked gorgeous against her shiny black hair. Her jeans showcased her slender but shapely legs.

"Do you sit and think here a lot?" he asked.

"Whenever I need to," she replied. "Where do you sit and think?" she asked curiously.

"I guess I do most of my thinking in my home office, although I don't usually just sit and think."

"Sitting someplace beautiful and just thinking is very good for the soul," she replied.

He laughed. "Then I suspect my soul needs a little tending."

She returned his laugh with musical tones of her own. "Then you'll have to work on that."

"I will. So, tell me about a typical day in Josie Cadieux's life," he said, wanting to learn everything he could about her. One thing he immediately noticed was her eyes were not jet black as he'd initially thought they were, but rather they were a deep gray with bright silver shards. Beautiful.

"I get up early and go out on the water to check my fishing lines and see what I've caught for the day. I bring what I caught back to my house where I put them in a holding cage and then just before sunset, I do that all over again. Once I have enough fish to take to market, I load them up in my truck and go into town."

"Who do you sell them to?" he asked curiously.

"I sell some of them directly to Marie Boujoulais at the Black Bayou Café and I also sell directly to Tremont's Restaurant. Then whatever is left over I take to Mike's Grocery store."

Mike's was the grocery store in the center of town that served everyone while Tremont's was a high-end restaurant where Jackson often ate with his friends.

"Sounds like a lot of work," he replied.

She shrugged her slender shoulders. "It's my life and I don't find it difficult at all. In fact, I think I have a wonderful life."

"What's so wonderful about it?" he asked.

"I make enough money to pay for my needs. I spend a lot of time outside in the beauty of the swamp. I can run when I feel like running or visit with friends when I feel like talking to somebody. I rarely have a worry in the world." She smiled. "Now tell me about a typical day in your life."

Her world sounded incredibly free and uncomplicated. As he told her about meetings, both in person and over FaceTime, he realized how boring he sounded. He rarely took any time off and when he did, he spent that time with people who were exactly like him.

"Your world sounds very complex," she observed when he was finished.

"I just now realized it is and maybe I need to make some changes. I'm certainly not enjoying my life much right now," he admitted. The only other person he'd ever shared his general unhappiness with was his friend Peyton. He was vaguely surprised that he'd shared this so easily with Josie, a woman he barely knew but felt surprisingly comfortable with.

"Life is too short to be unhappy," she replied.

"I agree with that. Sitting here and talking to a lovely woman certainly makes me happy," he replied.

She laughed. "Jackson, are you flirting with me?"

He grinned at her. "Maybe a little bit. I won't pour on the full force of my flirting power until I know for sure that you're single." He locked his gaze with hers. "So, have you decided yet? Are you single?"

Her lovely eyes drew him in as they sparkled brightly. Sure, he wanted to get to know her and there was no question that he was physically drawn to everything about her.

"Just for you, I've decided I'm single," she finally replied.

He smiled at her once again. "Josie, are you flirting with me?"

"Maybe just a little," she replied and then broke the eye contact with him. "So, tell me, are your parents still alive?"

"They are alive and well. I try to have dinner with them at least once a week or so," he replied.

"That's nice. Unfortunately, I lost my father two years ago and my mother a year and a half ago."

"I'm sorry for your loss. Were you close to them?"

"Extremely close," she replied. "In fact, we all lived together and they were my very best friends."

He heard the sadness that had crept into her voice and he reached his hand out and covered hers. "I'm really sorry," he said softly and then quickly pulled his hand back from hers, afraid of overstepping her boundaries.

"Thanks."

"So, tell me more about you. What's your favorite color? What sign are you? What's your favorite food?" he asked in an effort to turn the direction of their conversation to something lighter.

"My favorite color is deep purple and I'm a Libra. Right now, my favorite food is fish, because that's mostly all I've ever eaten in my life."

"So, you've never had a big juicy steak?"

"Never," she replied.

"Well, that definitely needs to be remedied," he said.

"I'll bet I can guess what your favorite color is," she said with a teasing light in her eyes.

"What do you think it is?" he asked.

"Green for money. And I would also guess that you're an Aries because they like to be number one and they're very ambitious."

He sniffed in exaggeration. "Uh, is that judgment I smell in the air?" he asked.

"No judgment," she quickly replied. "It was just an educated guess."

"I'll have you know my favorite color is blue and I'm actually a Cancer."

"A Cancer…hmm. Interesting," she replied. "I guess I still have a lot to learn about you."

He smiled. "And I want to learn a lot more about you."

"Are you flirting with me again, Mr. Fortier?"

He laughed. "Absolutely."

For the next hour or so, they talked about themselves and each other. He learned that she'd been homeschooled by her mother. Her mother must have done a good job for Jackson found Josie to be both intelligent and well-spoken.

She was quick-witted and had a wonderful sense of humor and he was positively enchanted by her. He'd never sat and talked to a woman before where he didn't feel the need to try to be clever and superficially charming.

He'd never felt like he could just let his guard down and be himself, but that's exactly what he was doing with Josie. She was wonderfully easy to talk to.

"I hope you're keeping yourself safe while you're out and about," he now said.

"I'm assuming you're talking about the Honey Island Swamp Monster." Her eyes darkened slightly.

"He's already killed three women," Jackson said.

"Don't I know it," she replied dryly. "But he's not a monster from the swamp. I believe it is a man from town who is somehow luring the women out of the swamp and to a place where he kills them and then leaves their bodies in an alleyway."

He looked at her in surprise. "I know it's a monster of the human kind, but I believe Chief Gravois thinks the killer is from the swamp."

A dry laugh escaped her. "As far as I'm concerned, Gravois does very little actual thinking for himself. And, of course, he believes the killer comes from here. He believes everything bad, everything evil, comes from the swamp. I doubt if he's even investigating the murders. After all, it's only women from the swamp who are being killed."

Bitterness was rife in her voice. She must have realized it for she laughed once again, the laughter now sounding a bit hollow and forced. "Sorry, I didn't mean to go on such a rant. But just don't get me started on Gravois."

"Don't apologize for telling me what you really think, and I agree with you that Gravois isn't much of a deep thinker. He's definitely the laziest man I've ever met," he replied. "I don't think he ever leaves his office unless he's going someplace where he's getting a free meal."

She laughed and then sobered, her gaze once again holding his. "So how much thought have you given to the murdered women?"

He thought about lying. He really wanted to put

his best foot forward with her, but he suspected she'd see right through his lie. "Not much," he admitted.

She nodded, as if she'd expected his answer.

"However," he continued, "maybe it's time me and some of my buddies put some pressure on Gravois about the murders."

A slow smile curved her lips and heated his blood. Damn but she was beautiful. "I would really appreciate that," she said.

"Consider it done," he replied.

"Do you like to fish?" she asked.

"I don't know. I've never been fishing."

"Really?" She looked at him in surprise. "Would you like to go fishing with me?"

He could think of a lot of things he'd like to do with her, but fishing certainly wasn't at the top of his list. Still, he recognized that she was bidding him an entry into her life with the invitation. "Sure, I'd like that."

"I have a sweet spot to sit and throw in a couple of lines and I've got a pole with your name written on it," she replied.

He looked at her nervously. "Aren't you afraid of the alligators?"

She laughed. "Let's just say I have a very healthy respect for them. Besides, usually when I'm fishing in that particular spot, Gator Broussard is around."

"He's the man who helped save Peyton's life."

"He is. Have you ever met him?"

"No," Jackson replied.

"Gator is older than dirt and loves catching gators. He even lost three of his fingers when he was fighting with one of the beasts."

"He sounds like a real character," Jackson said.

"Oh, he is. Maybe you'll get to meet him tomorrow morning."

He looked at her in surprise. "What's happening tomorrow morning?"

Her luscious lips curved upward again. "We're going fishing." She rose to her feet. "Why don't you meet me here around six thirty in the morning?"

"Okay," he replied, wondering exactly what he was getting himself into and yet excited to have another opportunity to spend time with her. He just hoped he didn't get eaten by a gator.

AFTER SHE LEFT JACKSON, Josie decided to pay Beau and Peyton a visit. She knew Peyton was good friends with Jackson and she wanted to know a little bit more about the man before she invested any more of her time with him.

Beau Boudreau and Peyton LaCroix shared a strange love story. They had been young lovers and then Beau, a swamp rat, had been accused and sent to prison for a murder he hadn't committed. He'd spent years in jail and once he got out, he returned to Black Bayou to clear his name.

By that time, Peyton had become a criminal defense lawyer. He'd enlisted her aid and, in the process, the two had realized they'd never stopped loving each other. The real killer had been exposed and despite

Peyton being a townie, she'd moved to the swamp to be with the man she loved. They now shared the best of both worlds, splitting their time between Beau's shanty in the swamp and her house in town.

It took Josie only a few minutes to reach their place. She knocked on the door and Peyton answered. "Hey, Peyton, do you mind a visitor for a few minutes?"

"Of course, we don't mind," Peyton replied. "Come on in." She opened the door and gestured Josie to the sofa. "Beau is off in town giving a bid on a deck."

"I really just wanted to talk to you," Josie replied as she sank down on the sofa. Beau had started his own carpentry business and, from what Josie had heard, he was doing quite well.

"Can I get you something to drink?" Peyton asked.

"No, thanks, I'm good."

Peyton sat in the chair facing the sofa in the small room. "So, what's up with you these days?"

"Not much, but I just got finished having a long visit with Jackson and I just wanted to ask you a few questions about him," Josie said.

Peyton's blue eyes widened. "You…and Jackson? Oh, that's a lovely thought. I'll tell you what you need to know about him. He's a wonderful man with a soft, kind heart. He would never hurt anyone so you'd be safe with him."

That was exactly the kind of information Josie had been looking for. "So, if the two of us were alone in my shanty, I shouldn't be afraid of him."

"Definitely not. I've known Jackson since we were

kids and I'm positive he would never ever hurt a woman." Peyton then laughed. "Don't get me wrong, he isn't a saint. Jackson can be sarcastic and superficial. He has a wicked sense of humor but he is also capable of making fun of himself."

Peyton leaned forward. "So, do you have plans to see him again?"

Josie grinned. "I'm taking him fishing in the morning."

Peyton's eyes opened wide in surprise and then she laughed again. "Oh, I wish I could be a fly in the air to see him in your element. I can't even believe it. It's going to be so amusing."

"We'll see if he really shows up in the morning," Josie replied.

"If he does show up, then it means he must like you a lot. I can't imagine Jackson stepping so far out of his comfort zone for just anyone."

"Thanks, Peyton." Josie got to her feet. "You answered the major questions I had about him."

Peyton stood as well. "Give him a chance, Josie, and try not to break his heart."

"That's certainly not in my plans," Josie replied.

Minutes later as she made her way back home, she replayed the conversation with Peyton in her head. The real thing she'd wanted…needed to know was if she would be safe with Jackson. While she respected Peyton's opinion, Josie wasn't about to stop wearing her knife when she was around him.

Besides, it wasn't just Jackson she had to worry

about. There was a serial killer loose, and he liked young swamp women. The townspeople had deemed the killer the Honey Island Swamp Monster, which was a real legend but not here around the Black Bayou.

According to the local gossip, the three women had been stabbed in the stomach and then mauled to death by some sort of animal claws. The victims had either been killed in the swamp and their bodies carried into town, or they had been lured out of the swamp and killed in town.

Josie didn't know anything else about the murders, but she knew enough to be wary when she was out and around. Hopefully, Jackson had been telling the truth when he'd told her he and his buddies would put some pressure on Gravois to solve the crimes. Three murders were definitely three too many.

According to Peyton, Jackson would really have to be interested in her to go fishing. It was going to be curious to see if he really showed up in the morning.

At six twenty the next morning, Josie sat on the dead tree trunk to await Jackson's arrival. She had with her two fishing poles, a tackle box and a container of nice fat worms.

She'd already run her lines that morning and gathered the fish she'd caught. Either later today or tomorrow, she needed to head into town to sell all of them.

She hadn't been sitting there long when she heard him coming. He crashed through the brush like a wild boar in a frenzy and she had to stifle a laugh as she heard a splash and then a deep string of curses.

He stepped into view and grinned at her with a shake of his head. "I can't seem to keep my right foot out of the water."

She laughed. "You'll get better in time. At least you're dressed appropriately for fishing this morning." He wore a pair of jeans that hugged his long legs and a royal blue T-shirt that stretched taut across his broad shoulders. The blue of the shirt was a perfect match for his sparkling eyes. Overall, he looked casual and very, very hot.

"I'm learning," he replied. "And you look very pretty today," he said. There was a warmth in his gaze that reinforced his words. The heat in his eyes leaped right into the pit of her stomach. It had been a very long time since a man had told her she looked pretty.

"Thanks," she replied and stood. "Are you ready to catch some fish?"

"As ready as I'll ever be," he replied.

She heard the slight trepidation in his voice. Still, she grabbed the two poles and handed him one of them, then she grabbed her tackle box and the can of worms. "Just follow me," she said.

"How long of a walk is it to your fishing spot?" he asked as they began the trek.

"About fifteen minutes or so," she replied and turned her head to glance back at him. "Are you okay?"

He flashed her a bright grin. "Lead on, oh, beautiful wood nymph."

She laughed and turned back around. The trail darkened and narrowed as they continued forward. She had to admit, he was a good sport to be doing this and she knew the only possible reason he would put himself through this was to spend more time with her.

He was looking like a live one…the perfect man for her to use in order to catch her assailant. Hopefully, he would eventually invite her outside of the swamp and into his world. But she didn't know if he would actually do that or not. Only time would tell.

The trail widened out once again and ahead was a small clearing that led to the dark water's edge. "We have arrived," she said. He stepped up next to her and looked around.

"We just throw our line in the water and we catch fish?"

"That's what we hope for." She sat down her fishing pole and opened up the can of worms. "Do you need me to bait your hook?"

"No, I think I can manage a little worm." As he stepped closer to grab the bait, his scent wafted to her. He smelled like minty soap, shaving cream and a fresh-scented cologne. It was a combination that drew her in.

They got their hooks baited, threw out the lines and then sat side by side on the ground. "Do you come here often?" he asked.

"About two or three times a week. I get most of my fish on the lines that I run. I just come out here to sit and relax."

"I can see where this would be relaxing," he replied. "You're making me realize I need to work in more down time for myself."

"What's holding you back from doing that? Do you need to keep working so hard to make more money? From what I've heard, you're already extremely wealthy."

He laughed. "I guess the gossipers stay busy in this town."

"Honestly, Jackson, I could care less about your net worth," she said.

He held her gaze for a long moment and then nodded. "If I thought your only interest in me was because of my wealth, I wouldn't be sitting here next to you right now."

She smiled at him. "I'm glad you're here."

He returned her smile. "I can't think of any place else I'd rather be. Actually, that's a lie. I can think of lots of other places I'd rather be with you next to me."

He jumped suddenly as the tip of his pole dipped. "Oh, I… I think I've got one." He got to his feet and she did as well.

"Give it a little jerk to set the hook," she said. "Reel it in, Jackson." She laughed as he reeled as fast as he could and finally got a good-size catfish on the shore.

"I did it," he said with a boyish joy. He set down

his pole, grabbed her into his arms and spun her around. "I caught my very first fish." He put her back down and took a step back from her. "I'm sorry. I got a little carried away."

"It's okay," she replied and laughed once again. "I definitely appreciate your enthusiasm." For just a moment, being held in his arms had felt wonderful. It had surprised her. She had thought she'd never want a man's arms around her again. "Uh…let's get that fish off the hook."

They sat and fished for about an hour, talking about all kinds of things. She shared stories from her childhood with him and he did the same. There was no question that they'd had different upbringings, but the common element was how much love they'd each enjoyed from their parents.

He caught another fish and she caught two and then they called it a day. She put the four fish on a hook to carry back to her place and then they headed out.

"I have to admit, I was dreading this yesterday, but this has been very nice," he said as he followed behind her on the narrow trail.

"It was nice to have your company this morning," she replied. It was true; she genuinely enjoyed him. He was funny and charming and easy to talk to. She almost felt bad that she just wanted to use him. Under different circumstances, she might have allowed herself to really like him.

However, if history had taught her anything at all, it was not to give her heart to a man from town.

Chapter Three

Jackson was definitely smitten. Josie made him feel more alive than he'd felt in a very long time. She intrigued him more than any other woman had in a very long time. He was excited about her and didn't want the day with her to end.

"What would you think about having dinner with me this evening at the café?" he asked once they'd reached the fallen tree trunk.

She looked at him in genuine surprise. "I think I would love that," she replied.

"Great. Why don't I meet you here about five thirty, then."

She smiled at him. "I'm not going to make you walk in to get me. How about I'll meet you in Vincent's parking lot at five thirty."

"That sounds perfect," he replied. "And this afternoon I intend to gather up a couple of my buddies and have a visit with Thomas Gravois. Hopefully, we'll be able to light a fire under him as far as these murders are concerned."

"Thank you, Jackson." She placed her hand on his arm, the touch immediately shooting a pleasant warmth through him. "I really appreciate it." She dropped her hand back to her side.

"Okay, then I'll just see you later this evening," he replied.

Minutes later, he was back in his car and headed to his townhouse. He was already anxious for the evening to come. He wanted to wine and dine her and maybe feed her her first bite of steak.

He hadn't been lying to her about having a visit with Gravois. He should have done it long before now. Three women brutally murdered should be on everyone's mind, no matter whether they were town women or from the swamp.

They were all women of Black Bayou and people should be up in arms about the vicious murders. He felt ashamed that it had taken Josie to really bring it to his full attention.

At one that afternoon, a knock sounded at his door. He answered and allowed in two of his friends. Brian Miller was a tall man with brown hair and green eyes. He also worked in real estate and owned properties all over the United States.

Lee Townsend had gone prematurely bald. His father had owned sugar cane fields and that was now Lee's business, making him a wealthy man.

"What's up?" Lee asked as Jackson ushered them into his living room.

"Sonny is supposed to be here, so I'll just wait for

him to arrive before I tell you why I called you all here," Jackson replied.

"That man is always late," Brian said.

"Yeah, he'll probably be fifteen minutes late to his own funeral," Lee replied with a laugh.

At that moment, another knock fell on the door and Jackson ushered in Sonny Landry. Sonny's father was a retired prosecuting attorney and Sonny had made his money working in the textiles industry.

The four men had grown up together. They had come from family wealth and worked hard to obtain their own money. They'd run the streets as young kids and dated most of the women in town.

They had all gone to different colleges, but wound up back in Black Bayou where they renewed their close friendships. There were two other men they were all close to, but Jackson hadn't been able to get a hold of them for this meeting.

Brian was married and had two young children and Lee was in the middle of a contentious divorce. Sonny, like Jackson, was single and dating around.

"So, what's up?" Sonny asked as he joined the other two on the large black sofa. "Have you called us all here for an emergency drinking session?"

Jackson laughed. "I don't know. Do we need one of those?"

"I definitely do," Lee said mournfully. "This divorce is killing me. Sherri's trying to take everything I own from me."

"You've got a good lawyer," Brian said. "You'll be

just fine." He turned his gaze to Jackson. "So, what's going on? Why'd you call us all here?"

"I'm hoping in the next few minutes you will all go to the police station with me where we can have a discussion about what our chief of police is doing to solve the swamp murders," Jackson said.

All three of them looked at him in surprise. "Since when do you care about what the law enforcement is doing in this town?" Lee asked.

"Since I met a beautiful woman who has opened my eyes to some important things," Jackson replied.

"A beautiful woman who lives in the swamp?" Brian asked.

Jackson nodded. "Her name is Josie and she's not only beautiful but she's also intelligent and interesting and has a great sense of humor."

"Hmm, somebody sounds quite infatuated," Sonny said with a grin. "When did you meet this paragon of womanhood?"

"Yesterday," Jackson replied. "But she's made me really think about the fact that three women have been brutally murdered and our chief of police doesn't seem to be working very hard to solve these killings," Jackson replied. "He hasn't even publicly addressed the issue."

"Gravois doesn't work too hard at anything but politicking and baby kissing," Lee said.

"Well, I want him to work harder at solving these murders," Jackson said firmly. "Will you all go with me to the station now so we can put some pressure on Gravois?"

"Sure, I'm in," Brian said.

"I'd love to," Lee replied. "Personally, I can't stand the man."

"Count me in, too," Sonny added.

About fifteen minutes later, they all pulled up and parked in front of the building that housed the Black Bayou Police Department and they all got out of their cars.

Jackson led the way into the small reception area where Officer Ryan Staub greeted them all with a touch of surprise. "What can I do for all you gentlemen this afternoon?" he asked.

"We'd like to speak to Chief Gravois. Is he in?" Jackson asked even though he knew what the answer would be. Gravois was always in.

"Yeah, he's here. Let me just go tell him you all are here to see him," Staub said. He got up from behind the counter and disappeared down a hallway only to return a few moments later. "Last door on the right," Staub said and opened the doorway that would allow all the men into the interior of the police station.

Once again, Jackson led the way down the narrow hallway. They passed several closed doors on either side of the hall and then reached Gravois's office. Jackson knocked twice on the door and then opened it.

Gravois sat behind his desk and didn't rise as they

all piled into the small office. "Well, this is a surprise. To what do I owe this unexpected visit?"

Thomas Gravois was a tall fit man. Although he was only in his mid-fifties, his dark hair was graying and there were deep lines around his blue eyes. He looked like a man who worked hard, but the gossip had always been that he was more than a little bit lazy. He had been married years ago but rumor had it his wife had left him. He lived alone in a house off Main Street.

"We're here as concerned citizens to check on the progress of the murder investigations of the three women," Jackson said.

Gravois raised an eyebrow in obvious surprise. He then leaned back in his chair and released an audible sigh. "Unfortunately, there hasn't been much forward progress on those cases. I'll tell you what, those swamp people are tight-knit and they aren't talking to me or any of my officers."

"Are you still interrogating people to see if there were any witnesses to the crimes?" Lee asked.

"There's really no point, like I said, they are all closed off and not talking," Gravois said. "I think they're protecting one of their own."

"Surely, there was some blood evidence," Brain said. "I heard their faces were ripped off. The perp had to have been covered in tons of blood. Have you found footprints or handprints of any kind?"

"Nothing. It was like a ghost wild animal killed them and left no prints or other evidence behind,"

Gravois replied. "I think it's obvious somebody from the swamp is responsible."

"And why is that so obvious?" Jackson asked, his temper flaring just a bit.

"You know, most of those people are nothing more than uneducated pests," Gravois replied.

Jackson knew there was a general prejudice amidst the townspeople against the people who lived in the swamp, but for an elected official to espouse something like that was not only shocking and unprofessional, but it also showed what an uneducated swine Gravois was.

"It wasn't anyone from the swamp who tried to kill Peyton LaCroix, it was a well-respected business man from town," Jackson said.

Jack Fontenot, a man who owned a successful construction company had not only framed his best friend, Beau Boudreau, for the murder of a young woman, but when Peyton's investigation into that crime got too hot, Fontenot had gone after Peyton. Thankfully, she'd survived the attack and Jack was in jail, awaiting trial on charges that would probably send him away for the rest of his life.

"Look, I'm doing the best I can to solve these murders. You boys know I'm shorthanded and without any real clues they've been difficult to investigate." Gravois's voice turned slightly whiny.

"Surely, you have enough in the coffers to hire another officer or two, if that's what you need to do," Brian said.

"Yeah, I seem to remember you got a huge budget passed at the beginning of the year," Lee added.

"Nobody around here has applied for a job and I don't see anyone coming to this small town to live and work," Gravois said.

"You're full of a lot of excuses," Jackson said. "Isn't this an election year?"

Gravois's face reddened and his eyes narrowed in obvious anger. "I told you all I'm doing the very best that I can and that's all I can do."

"Maybe you should put some ads in the papers in New Orleans and some of the surrounding areas and see if you can get another officer or two to come in and help with the investigation," Sonny suggested.

"We'd just like to see more forward progress in these cases," Jackson said.

"Believe me, we all want the same thing," Gravois replied as he stood. "I appreciate you all stopping in here and letting me know your concerns." It was an obvious dismissal.

Minutes later, the four men stood next to Jackson's car. "Thanks for coming with me," Jackson said to his friends.

"No problem. Gravois is a man I'd love to kick in his lazy, prejudice ass," Brian said.

"That makes two of us," Lee replied. "I can't believe what he said about the people from the swamp."

"I'm hoping that now that he knows we're looking at him, he'll get up off his chair and do a true investigation of these murders," Jackson replied. "It's past time this killer is caught. Anyway, thanks again for all the support."

"Anytime," Lee replied and the others echoed that sentiment.

Later as Jackson drove home, he eagerly anticipated the evening to come with Josie. He was excited to see her again and to tell her about the conversation with Gravois. He was ashamed that it had taken him this long to have the talk with the police chief and he would tell her that, too.

JOSIE STOOD IN front of the floor-length mirror on the back of her closet door and pronounced herself ready to go. The Black Bayou Café was casual dining and so she wore a nice pair of jeans and a royal blue fitted long-sleeved blouse.

The jeans fit her snugly and showcased not only her slender waist but also her long legs. The blouse had a V-neck that hinted at her cleavage but didn't give too much away.

She'd pulled her hair back at the nape of her neck and secured it with a gold clasp and small gold hoop earrings hung from her ears. She'd gone heavy on the mascara and dusted her cheeks with a wisp of blush.

"This is as good as it gets," she said to the reflection in the mirror and then turned and left her bedroom.

She went into the living room and sank down on the sofa. It was a little too early for her to make her way to Vincent's parking lot to meet Jackson. She leaned back and took a couple of deep breaths to calm the nervous energy that danced inside her.

Tonight would be her very first time going to the café with a date. In all the time she had dated Gentry O'Connal, a man from town, he'd never taken her out of the swamp. Of course, she hadn't cared because she'd believed herself to be completely in love with Gentry, and she'd thought he loved her, too.

She'd been such a fool. That had been a little less than a year and a half ago and the whole experience with him had built a hard shield around her heart. But she couldn't help but be excited about Jackson.

This night was the first in her plan to catch her assailant. If she could keep Jackson interested in her, then he might invite her to something more than the café, someplace where she would meet a lot of his friends and acquaintances. Among those men, her attacker was hiding and she was determined to use Jackson to find him.

With this thought in mind, she got up from the sofa and left her shanty. As she walked slowly down the path, she drew in the scent and sounds of the surrounding swamp. This was her home and she couldn't imagine living any place else. The swamp calmed her and gave her peace.

The minute she stepped out of the marsh, she saw him waiting for her. His dark blue car was sleek and shiny and when he saw her, he immediately got out from behind the steering wheel. He wore a pair of jeans and a royal blue polo shirt that once again showed off his broad shoulders.

"Hi, beautiful," he said with a wide smile.

"Hi yourself," she replied, shocked by the wild jump in her heartbeat and the pool of warmth that filled the pit of her stomach at the sight of him.

He went around the car to the passenger side and opened the door for her. "Thank you, sir," she said and slid into the seat.

The interior smelled of leather cleaner and his pleasant fresh-scented cologne. She watched as he walked around the car to the driver side.

She was definitely attracted to him. But the fact that she found him extremely pleasing to the eyes didn't mean she was going to put her heart on the line. She reminded herself that she was on a mission and nothing more. She would absolutely not allow herself to like him too much.

He got in the car, started the engine and then turned to look at her. "You look positively gorgeous this evening," he said.

A warmth filled her cheeks. "Thank you."

He put the car into gear and took off. "Are you hungry?"

"Starving," she admitted.

"I'm determined tonight to get you to take your first bite of a nice medium-rare steak."

She laughed. "I'm always willing to try new things. Have you ever had fish stew?"

"No, I can't say I have," he replied.

"Then maybe tomorrow night you could come to my place and I'll make you some fish stew."

He flashed her a quick glance. "Thank you, I'd really like that."

Inviting him into her personal space was a big deal. The only other men who had ever been there had been her father and then Gentry. But she was willing to invite him in if it got him to take her out around town more.

As he continued the quick drive to the café, they only had time to talk about the weather before he was parking in front of the eating establishment. There was a possibility of storms later that night but when they got out of the car, the skies were clear.

Josie had only been in the Black Bayou Café once as a diner and that had been about a year ago when she and a girlfriend from the swamp had eaten lunch here. However, when she'd been a child, she'd often hung out in the kitchen while her mother visited with Marie Boujoulais, the owner of the café. The two women had been good friends for many years.

Nothing much had changed since then. The walls were painted a cheerful yellow and two of them had hand-painted murals, one of Main Street and one of cypress trees dripping with Spanish moss.

Jackson took her by the elbow and led her to one of the booths toward the back of the place. As they passed the occupied booths and tables, most of the people greeted Jackson with a friendly nod or quick pleasantries. It was obvious he was well-liked and respected in the small town.

They reached their spot and she slid in on one side of the booth and he sat across from her. The booth had a window that looked out on Main Street. The lighting inside was fairly low and even with the big window, the space felt rather intimate.

He smiled at her, his eyes filled with a pleasant warmth. "Did I tell you that you look gorgeous this evening?"

She returned his smile. "You told me something like that."

"Well, let me say it again, you look absolutely beautiful this evening."

"My, my, Mr. Fortier, you'll turn my head with all that sweet talk."

"Aside from your physical beauty, I like you, Josie. I like your intelligence and your sense of humor. I like that you're thoughtful and make me think about how superficial my life has become."

"I like you, too, Jackson. The fact that you're questioning anything about your life shows me that you aren't superficial at all."

The conversation was interrupted by the arrival of their waitress. "Can you give us just a minute or two," Jackson asked the perky blonde who wore a name tag identifying her as Heidi.

"Sure, how about I take care of your drink orders and then I'll be back for your dinner orders," she said.

"Perfect." Jackson looked at Josie. She ordered a sweet tea and he did the same. Once Heidi left the booth, Jackson and Josie looked at the menus.

By the time their drinks were delivered, they were ready to order. She got the grilled salmon and he ordered a rib eye. "Guess what I did this afternoon," he said once Heidi had left with their orders.

God, he was hot with his blue long-lashed eyes shining so brightly. His lips looked firm yet soft and she found herself wondering what it would be like to kiss him. She had a feeling he would probably be a good kisser. She was surprised by the quick fire of sexual desire for him. It was the first time she'd felt anything like this since her attack. It felt healthy and good, making her realize she was hopefully moving beyond the trauma.

"Josie?"

"Oh, sorry," she replied, realizing she'd zoned out for a moment. Why on earth would she care how he kissed? Jeez, what was wrong with her? "So, what did you do this afternoon?"

"Me and three of my buddies went to have a chat with Gravois."

She stared at him for a long moment. He'd told her he intended to do it, but she honestly hadn't believed him. She was ridiculously pleased that he had followed through. "What did he have to say?" she asked.

"He said the investigation was going nowhere because you swamp people were tight-knit and unwilling to answer any questions. He also said he was certain the guilty party is from the swamp because of the heinous nature of the crimes."

"He's totally vile," Josie said. There were a lot more stronger words that she'd have liked to use to describe the man, but she swallowed hard against them.

"I agree. But he now knows he's got eyes on him. Hopefully, we put enough pressure on him that he'll do his damn job and really work hard to solve the murders."

She reached across the table and touched the back of his hand. "Thank you so much, Jackson." She quickly pulled her hand back, surprised by the warmth that momentarily flooded through her at the simple touch.

What was wrong with her? She hadn't even thought about a man in almost a year and yet there was no denying that Jackson was sparking something deep inside her, something slightly exciting and definitely hot. It was also something dangerous. She was definitely going to have to hang on to her emotions where he was concerned.

Their meals arrived and as they began to eat, they talked more about their families. She was surprised to learn that Jackson had a sister. Her name was Gwen and she was married and lived in Houston, Texas.

"She's five years older than me and we weren't really that close growing up," Jackson now said.

"Did you get closer when you got older?" she asked curiously.

"We were fairly close when we were in our twenties, but then she met her husband and they moved to Houston for his job. She now has three kids and we occasionally text back and forth but she leads a pretty busy life."

"Speaking of children, would you like to have any?" she asked.

"Sure, in a perfect world I'd like to be married and have a couple of kids. But so far, I've been stuck on the married part. But I'm thinking maybe my luck has changed in that department." He cast her that charming warm grin that made her heart inexplicably dance in her chest. "What about you? Do you want kids?"

"In a perfect world if I found the perfect man, then yes, I'd like to have children," she replied.

For the next few minutes, they fell silent and focused on their food. The fish was delicious and the fried potatoes and greens that had come with it were also good.

"Have you ever eaten any kind of meat?" he asked when they were halfway through the meal.

"My mother fixed pork chops for us a couple of times and I've had the occasional ham and cheese sandwich at Big Larry's, but that's it." Big Larry's was a popular sandwich and burger joint in town.

"Then I must introduce you to steak, and this one is particularly juicy and flavorful." He cut off a piece of his and then reached across the table with the steak bite on his fork.

It felt oddly intimate for her to lean forward and take the meat off his utensil with her mouth, but that's exactly what she did. It was just as he'd described it…juicy and flavorful.

"What do you think?" he asked as he leaned back in his seat.

She finished chewing and swallowed and then replied, "It's really good."

"So, if I invited you to my place for a barbecue of steaks, then you would come and eat the steak?"

She laughed. "Yes, I would come and eat whatever you prepared for me."

"Then we'll have to plan it for one night."

Things were moving very fast with him and yet she didn't want to slow it down. The more time she spent with him, especially in public, the more opportunities she might have to meet her attacker.

More than once while they were eating, people stopped by their booth to visit with him for just a minute. She paid special attention to each male he introduced her to, but she knew by their voices that none of them so far were the man she sought.

Once they finished the meal, Jackson insisted they have dessert and coffee. She ordered a slice of chocolate cake and he got the apple crisp.

As they waited for it, she glanced out the window, but it was dark enough outside now that she couldn't see anything. She looked back at Jackson. "Even though it's relatively early, it looks like it's really gotten dark outside."

"Yeah, the weathermen forecasted clouds and rain overnight and into tomorrow," he replied.

"Then maybe you won't want to come to my place tomorrow evening for fish stew," she replied.

"Trying to back out on me, Josie?" he asked with a teasing sparkle in his eyes.

She laughed. "No, not at all. I was just thinking about you."

The twinkle left his eyes as his gaze lingered on her. "Honestly, Josie, I would walk through a hurricane to spend more time with you."

His words found a softness in her heart that she hadn't realized still existed. He was moving very quickly with her. Surely, he hadn't come to that depth of caring about her yet. Still, his words were very nice to hear.

She'd believed her ordeal with Gentry had hardened everything inside her and the assault had taken any softness that had been left behind.

Jackson was definitely getting to her and she couldn't allow that. She refused to allow another man to ever hurt her again.

HE SAW THEM in the café window and momentarily froze in his tracks. One of his best friends and the woman he had attacked apparently having dinner together. Jesus, what was Jackson doing with her? How in the hell had the two of them hooked up?

He quickly crossed the street and headed to his car, his head screaming a wild cacophony of thoughts. Had she told Jackson about that night when a wildness and a rage had filled him? Had she told him about the assault on her that had happened months ago?

It was obvious she hadn't been able to identify him, at least by name. Otherwise, Gravois would have arrested him by now. The bag he'd pulled over her head had prevented her from seeing him…at least that's what he hoped.

But what if she had gotten a brief glance of him? What if she saw him again in a different setting? Would she be able to identify him as her attacker? What if she recognized his voice again? Damn, he should have never said anything to her on that night, but he hadn't been able to help himself.

He got into his car and grabbed the steering wheel tightly in order to halt the violent shaking of his hands. He closed his eyes and tried to remember all the details of that night.

He'd left his place filled with a rage that knew no boundaries. He'd like to think he hadn't planned what happened, but he knew in his heart that wasn't true.

Otherwise, why had he grabbed the bag from his garage? Why had he headed to the swamp to see whom he might encounter? He now knew from Jackson that her name was Josie, but he hadn't known it that night. He hadn't specifically targeted her; she was just the first female to come into his sights.

Her back had been toward him and it had been a perfect storm. He'd bagged her and then tagged her. He had his way with her and then ran, filled with a self-hatred but also empty of the enormous rage that had initially driven him away from home.

He hadn't been back to the swamp since then, although he'd been tempted on several different occasions when his anger had reached a boiling point. He'd managed that anger on those occasions by going to the Voodoo Lounge, a dive bar on the west side of town. He'd managed to drown his anger in a bottle of gin.

He glanced back toward the café. He was a hell of a businessman and had worked hard to gain his place in society. One thing was certain, there was no way in hell he was going to let a swamp slut take him down.

Chapter Four

Josie had swept the floors and dusted all the surfaces in her home. The place was completely clean and as far as she was concerned, it looked homey and inviting.

She had cans of soda, a couple of beers and bottled water on ice to go with the evening meal. The fish stew was simmering on the electric burner and she'd bought fresh-baked corn bread and coleslaw at the store that day.

She now sank down on the sofa to wait for the time to meet Jackson at their tree trunk and walk him to her shanty. She could hear the slight hum of her generator working and the air smelled of fish and tomatoes and onions, along with the other spices she'd used to make the savory stew.

He'd kissed her last night. It had been a quick sweet kiss at the end of the night that surprisingly had made her want more from him.

There had been moments during their meal last night where she'd forgotten that she had an ulterior motive for being with him. There were moments when she'd just found herself enjoying his company as any woman might enjoy a date with a handsome charming man.

Their conversation had flowed easily and yet she'd experienced a simmering warmth in the pit of her that was both pleasant and disturbing.

Maybe he was the wrong man for her to attempt to use. So far, he seemed so nice and kind. But if she didn't use him, then how long would she have to wait for another man of his social stature to wander into the swamp?

No, Jackson was perfect and she just needed to stuff any personal feelings she had for him aside. She needed him to put her in a position to find her assailant and nothing more. Still, she couldn't help but wonder what it would be like if he pulled her into his arms and gave her a real long deep kiss.

She jumped up from the sofa and walked into the bathroom to take a last look at herself. The sleeveless red blouse cinched her waist and looked nice with her jeans. Once again, she'd clasped her long hair back at the nape of her neck. With a glance at the time, she left the bathroom, turned off the hot plate under the stew and then headed for the door. It was time to go pick up her date.

As always, when she walked through the swamp with its scents and vivid colors surrounding her, her head cleared of everything and she was at peace.

Jackson was waiting for her on the tree trunk and

when he caught sight of her, a wide smile curved his lips. Damn his smile, for it created that crazy heat to swirl around deep inside her.

"Hey, handsome. What are you doing hanging out in these parts of the woods," she said in greeting.

He rose from the log. "I'm just sitting here, hoping a beautiful young woman will come along and take me with her for a delicious home-cooked meal."

"You just happen to be in luck. I have a nice stew simmering at my place and my table is set for two," she replied. She reached her hand out for his. "Come on, I'll take you there."

As she led him into the depths of the swamp to reach her shanty, they talked about the heavy cloud cover portending rain and the fact that he had eaten very little at lunch in anticipation of her fish stew.

She suspected part of his chatter was to mask his tension as she led him deeper into the wildness. She knew he hadn't been this deep into the swamp before and he would probably not be able to find her place again on his own.

They finally reached her home. They crossed the bridge that would lead up to her porch and then she dropped his hand. "Welcome to my humble abode," she said as they walked into the front door.

He stopped inside the threshold and looked around. She followed his gaze. The dark brown sofa held a couple of turquoise and yellow throw pillows. A matching brown chair sat opposite it. Against one wall was the small potbellied stove with cookware on top.

The living room flowed into the kitchen area that had just enough space for a small table and chairs. She'd used two white plates and turquoise cloth napkins for the meal.

"This is nice," he said. "Very homey, and something smells delicious."

"That would be your dinner." She walked over to the hot plate and turned it back on to warm up the stew. "Would you like a cold beer or soda while we wait for this to warm up?"

"A beer sounds good. Are you going to have one with me?"

"Sure." She plucked the two beers out of the ice chest and handed him one. "Sit down and relax." She gestured to the sofa. He sank down on one end and she sat on the other. Together they cracked open their beers.

He took a deep drink and then smiled at her. "So, how has your day been?"

"Like most of them are, fairly quiet. I did my fish run this morning and then just pretty much puttered around here until noon and then I made a run to the grocery store and came home to fix the stew. What about you?"

"I did some paperwork this morning and then had a light lunch with a couple of my friends and now I'm here with you." He took another drink and scooted closer to her. "This is definitely the best part of my day."

"You are quite a charmer, Mr. Fancy Pants," she replied.

He laughed. "I don't know about that, but I do know that it's nice to see where you live. Now when I think of you, I'll envision you snuggled among the turquoise and yellow pillows on the sofa as the frogs croak and the fish jump just outside your front door."

"So, tell me about your townhouse so I can envision you there," she said.

"I'll do one better. How about Friday night I take you there so you can see it for yourself," he said. "I'll grill you a nice steak for dinner. Would you be up for that?"

"I would definitely be up for that," she replied.

"Good." His eyes shone with a light that shot a small shiver up her spine. It was an intimate gaze that made her feel as if he were both seducing her and probing into the very depths of her soul.

"Excuse me for a minute." She jumped up from the sofa and went to stir the stew. *Remember, you're just using him...nothing more*, a little voice reminded her. Seeing that the stew was warm, she placed the coleslaw, the corn bread and the butter on the table and then got two bowls down from the cabinet. "This is ready if you are," she said.

He picked up his beer and stood. "Does it matter which seat I take?"

"It doesn't matter at all," she replied.

As he sat, she dipped up the stew in the bowls and added them to the table. "This looks really good," he said and unfolded the napkin on his lap.

"I hope you like it. It's my mother's recipe," she

replied. "We had it a lot as I was growing up, but I don't fix it very often now."

She watched as he took a spoonful of the stew and popped it into his mouth. He chewed for a moment, swallowed and then grinned at her. "Josie, this is absolutely delicious."

She expelled a small sigh of relief. "I'm so glad you like it. And help yourself to the corn bread and slaw."

"Thanks. So, tell me more about your mother. Did she enjoy cooking?"

"She did, although she cooked almost every meal on the potbellied stove while I broke down and bought an electric stovetop burner, which serves me well."

"Tell me something else about your parents."

The meal passed pleasantly with her reminiscing about her parents and then him sharing more about his own parents.

"My parents are still madly in love with each other and they are also best friends," he said. "They've been a really good role model for me on how a relationship should work."

"Same with my parents," she replied. "They were still crazy in love with each other until the day they died. I envision them right now in heaven sitting on a sofa and holding hands."

"That's a nice vision and that's the kind of relationship I'd like to have," Jackson said.

"Me, too," she agreed although she didn't really believe she'd ever find that kind of love for herself.

She'd thought she'd found it with Gentry but that certainly hadn't panned out.

Before long, the meal was over and she insisted they leave the cleanup for later and instead move back to the sofa for more conversation.

It felt good to have him here with her. She had to admit that there were times when she got lonely and missed having somebody to talk to…somebody to share things with. It was especially lonely in the hours between dinnertime and bedtime.

Although she had several girlfriends who lived nearby and a couple of male friends as well, at the end of the day they weren't what she wanted. She didn't want casual friendships to fill that time. She yearned for somebody special.

There was no question that there was something exciting about sitting on the sofa with Jackson. His gaze on her was so intent and held the undeniable spark of physical attraction. It was exciting and just a little bit frightening because she felt an undeniable spark of attraction to him.

Was he the same kind of man as Gentry? Was he only after a quick roll in the hay with a swamp woman? Was he just a townie looking for something that was a bit taboo and exotic? That's what most town men who ventured into the swamp were looking for.

No, she couldn't believe that about Jackson. He'd already treated her with more respect than Gentry ever had. Gentry had never taken her anywhere in public. Jackson had taken her to the café and he'd acted proud to be seen out in public with her. That was proof in and of itself that Jackson was a different kind of man from Gentry.

They continued talking until darkness had fallen outside and it was time for her to take him to the place where he could make his way back to his car. She grabbed a flashlight from a kitchen cabinet, knowing that he would feel more comfortable with a light even though she didn't necessarily need it.

The minute they stepped out of her door, the scent of impending rain hung heavy in the air. "We should probably hurry so you don't get wet," she said.

"I'd rather get wet than hurry and accidentally fall into the deep dark waters of the swamp," he replied. "I'm convinced I'd be a tasty morsel for some alligator lurking nearby."

She laughed. "I promise I won't let you fall into the water and get eaten by a gator."

Together they took off, her leading the way and him following her closely behind. The swamp breathed heavily all around them with the sounds of night creatures awakening and day creatures nestling in for the night. A heavy breeze whistled through the treetops as tousled leaves added to the myriad sounds.

She kept the flashlight directed to the ground more for Jackson's benefit than her own. She knew these paths as well as she knew her own heartbeat but tonight there wasn't even a ray of moonlight to illuminate the paths. The sky was as dark as the swamp waters that surrounded them.

It took only a few minutes for them to reach the fallen tree trunk where they always met. "I can't tell you how much I enjoyed both the meal and the company," he said as they stopped.

"It's been a real pleasure, Jackson," she replied. Her heart picked up its pace as he took a couple of steps closer to her.

"Thank you for sharing your home with me." He took another step forward and now stood so close to her that she could feel his warm breath on her face.

"You're welcome."

"Josie, can I kiss you good-night?"

"I… I'd like that." She was surprised to realize it was true. She wanted him to kiss her again and she hoped it was more than the little peck they had shared the night before.

She leaned slightly forward and he gathered her into his arms. He took her lips with his, plying hers with an incendiary heat that she couldn't help but answer with a fire of her own.

He deepened the kiss, his tongue dancing into battle with hers as he drew her closer against him. It surprised her, the fact that she felt undeniably safe in his arms…so safe with him.

Yet at this very moment, a delicious desire flooded through her veins. She wanted him. She wanted more than his kisses and that shook her up. She'd believed after the assault that she'd never want a man again.

At the very moment she considered bringing him back to her cabin to finish what they'd started, a flash of lightning rent the sky, followed by a deafening boom of thunder.

She sprung back from him, the mood shattered by the vivid show of nature. "I have to tell you, Josie, when I kiss you, I see fireworks in the sky and I feel the earth move under my feet," he said.

She laughed at his silliness. "You'd better get out of here before you feel the rain of the gods soaking your butt."

He returned her laugh. "Good night, Josie."

"'Night, Jackson."

She watched as he turned and headed down the path that would take him back to his car in Vincent's parking lot, then she pivoted to go back home.

Lightning once again slashed through the darkness with another boom of thunder afterward. The minute the thunder quieted, she heard it…the slap of footsteps close behind her.

It was possible it was Gator Brossard. The old man was known to wander about in the darkness of the swamp no matter what the time or weather. However, the person was moving far too quickly to be Gator.

She cast a quick glance over her shoulder and gasped. A man wearing a ski mask over his head was gaining on her. Who? Wh-what did he want? Whatever he wanted, it couldn't be good given his face covering. Her heart accelerated and she grabbed the knife sheath from her waistband and pulled out her knife.

She certainly didn't want to confront the man. However, if she had to, she'd use her knife to defend herself.

Instead, she picked up her pace. She ran as fast as it was possible into the very depths of the swamp. The last thing she wanted to do was lead this person to her shanty.

Branches slapped at her and Spanish moss dripped down from the trees, half-blinding her as she raced for her life. And it did feel like she was running for her life. The masked man definitely screamed to her of imminent danger.

A gasp escaped her as a light filled the area. Oh, God, the person chasing her had turned on a flashlight. Up until now, she had hoped to outrun him and disappear into the darkness. But he was gaining on her and now he could see her as she ran.

She left the path, zigzagging through the thicket. Thank God she knew almost every inch of the swamp. Her breaths came in deep gasps as she frantically bobbed and weaved through the thicket.

Tree limbs clawed at her and roots in the ground tried to trip her up. The brush came alive with animals trying to escape her wild dash and the sound of wild boars rooting nearby added to her fear.

The lightning overhead was her enemy as it flashed a bright illumination and the thunder only added to the madness of her wild race through the marshland.

She didn't know how long she ran before she was utterly breathless. Panting, she realized she needed to stop and take a breath. She couldn't go on running as she was completely out of gas. But he was still somewhere behind her. Frantically, she looked around for a good hiding place.

Cautiously, she stepped down into the murky water near her and around a big knobby cypress tree. Grateful that it wasn't too deep and she didn't see any gators around, she crouched down and waited. Her heart still banged with frantic beats as she drank in deep gulps of air as quietly as possible.

She drew in a deep breath and held it as the light appeared flashing all around. Oh, he was definitely hunting for her. Was he the same person who had attacked her almost a year ago? Or was he the Honey Island Swamp Monster looking for his next victim? Either way, she definitely didn't want to be found.

She pulled her body tight against the tree root and slid even deeper into the water in an effort to stay hidden. The light continued to flash all around as she held her breath. Thankfully, it didn't find her. She hoped the next flash of lightning wouldn't bring her into his view.

After several long minutes, the person turned and headed away from her. She slowly expelled her breath. She waited a long time before she finally moved from her position and slowly rose from the water.

Her heart had not stopped its frenzied beat and it continued to beat that way as she slowly made her way to her shanty. She no longer heard footsteps behind her and was relatively certain she had lost him.

Still, once her home was in her sights, she remained hidden in the brush nearby as she watched it for several long minutes. She needed to make sure the person who had chased her hadn't somehow found her shanty and waited for her there.

Seeing nobody in the area, she quickly ran across the bridge and to the front door. Once inside she locked the door and then immediately ran to look all around. Thankfully, she was alone. She hurried over to the window and peered out. Nothing stirred and the frogs had resumed their croaking melodies, which indicated to her that nobody was around.

She finally sank down on her sofa and began to cry. The residual fear fell from her in deep sobs. She eventually stopped crying. Even though she was soaking wet, she didn't move from her seat as the horrifying event whirled around and around in her head.

Who had he been? There was no question that he'd had bad intentions with the ski mask hiding his face. Had he merely been looking for somebody… anybody to prey on or had he been hunting for her specifically? That thought terrified her even more.

THOUGHTS OF JOSIE filled Jackson's head from the moment he woke up the next day. He showered and went into his home office to get some paperwork done, but he found it hard to concentrate as all he could think of was her.

He wasn't sure what he'd been expecting, but he'd found her home small, but both charming and inviting. The fish stew she had prepared was delicious, but it was definitely the fire of their goodbye kiss that had stayed with him.

He wanted her. He wanted her not just because her body had fit so perfectly against his own and not just because her kiss had shot flames of desire through him, but also because he liked her. In fact, he thought he might be falling in love with her.

It sounded completely crazy after having known her for such a short period of time, but he'd spent more time with her in the past week than he'd spent with the last woman he had dated for three months.

Josie touched him on all levels. Intellectually, she challenged him and emotionally she stirred him in ways no woman had ever done before. And then there was the physical desire he felt for her and if the kiss they'd shared was any indication, she desired him, too.

It felt like she was the woman he'd been searching for in his life. He'd dated so many women in the past and had been unable to find the one who fit him so perfectly. So far, Josie was the woman who fit him perfectly.

He hated the fact that he wouldn't see her again until tomorrow night. He hated even more that she didn't own a cell phone so he could call her when they were apart. She'd told him she'd never felt the need for a phone before and had no plans to ever get one in the future.

Last night as they'd walked back to the tree trunk from her place, they'd made arrangements for him to meet her in Vincent's parking lot Friday night at six o'clock.

He didn't know how long he'd been sitting there, staring off into space with thoughts of her when his phone rang. The caller ID showed him it was Lee. "Hey, man, what's up?" he asked.

"I was wondering if you want to meet me for lunch today at Tremont's. I just got out of a court hearing and I'm totally depressed."

Jackson looked at his watch, shocked to realize it was already almost eleven o'clock. "Sure, I can meet you."

"Great. How about noon?"

"Sounds perfect, I'll be there," Jackson replied.

It was quarter to twelve when Jackson pulled up in the parking lot of Tremont's. The upscale restaurant was housed in a sleek black and gray building with the name in large silver lettering.

He got out of his car and went inside where Layla Brighton stood at the hostess stand. "Good afternoon, Mr. Fortier," she greeted him with a big smile.

"Hi, Layla, are you staying out of trouble?"

The young woman laughed. "I'm definitely trying. Are you dining alone today or meeting other people?"

"I think it's just two of us today. Lee Townsend is meeting me and should be here shortly."

She picked up two menus. "If you'll follow me, I'll get you seated. Booth or table?"

"I always prefer a booth," he replied.

She led him to the seat located halfway toward the back. "Perfect," he said as he slid into the side facing the door.

"A waitress will be with you shortly," she said as she set the menus on the table. "And I'll bring Mr. Townsend back as soon as he arrives."

"Thanks, Layla," he replied.

He settled into the booth and looked around. He waved and nodded at several people he knew and at that moment a waitress arrived to take his drink order.

She'd just delivered his glass of sweet tea when Lee showed up. He slid in across from Jackson and ordered a scotch and soda from the waitress.

"Bad morning?" Jackson asked.

Lee shook his head with a deep frown. "The worst. Sherri has gone completely, money-hungry crazy. She's not only asking for the house to be mortgage-free and put in her name, but she's also asking for an astronomically high amount of money monthly for alimony."

"Thank God the two of you don't have kids," Jackson said.

"I don't even want to think what that would have cost me, but Sherri never wanted to have any children. Just tell me, what woman really needs nine thousand dollars a month to live? Nine thousand dollars. I mean, does mascara and hair spray really cost that much a month?"

Jackson couldn't help but laugh. "Surely, your lawyer is going to fight everything."

"He is, but I was really hoping we could do all this amicably and reasonably, but she's going for my throat. All I ever did to her was love her." He stopped as the waitress arrived with his drink and then took their food orders.

"I didn't even want the divorce," Lee continued once the waitress was gone. "It was all her idea. She's the one who decided to leave me."

"I'm sorry this is all going to be so painful for you," Jackson said.

Lee took a sip of his drink and then shook his head once again. "We were married for eight years. You think you know somebody but when the chips are down, the person you thought you knew turns into a stranger. Anyway, enough of my sob story, how are things going with you?"

"Really good."

"You still seeing that swamp woman?"

"Josie…her name is Josie and yes I am," Jackson replied. "In fact, I'm more than already a little bit crazy about her."

"Wow, that was fast."

"I know, right? But so far things are going great between us," Jackson said.

"Are you planning on bringing her to Mrs. Patty's gala next weekend?" Lee asked.

"I'd forgotten all about the gala," Jackson replied with a frown. About twice a year Patty Bardot, a wealthy older widow, opened up her home for a fancy gala. These parties were considered must-not-miss social events.

"Yes, I'll definitely bring Josie if she'll come with me," Jackson said, excited by the very thought. He didn't know if Josie would have an appropriate dress to wear to the fancy event but, if necessary, he would provide her with whatever she needed to be his date for the big gala.

"That will make a lot of people talk, you bringing a woman from the swamp," Lee replied. "And it will definitely tick off all the women in town who have been chasing you for years."

Jackson laughed. "I don't give a damn about people talking about me and I've dated most all the eligible women in town and never found a connection. The heart wants what the heart wants and right now my heart wants Josie."

"I never thought I'd see the day that you would be off the market because of a swamp woman," Lee said.

"Stop calling her that," Jackson said with an irritated tone. "The swamp is just the place where she lives. It has nothing to do with who she is. She's Josie, period."

Lee raised an eyebrow. "Oh, you definitely have it bad for her."

At that moment, their lunch was delivered. Jackson had ordered a club sandwich and Lee had ordered a burger. As they ate, their conversation lightened up. They talked about work and the storm that had moved through overnight and some of the news headlines of the day.

Finally, the conversation returned once again to Lee's divorce. "I'm just so damned angry about it all," he said. "And I don't know what to do with all this rage I have built up inside me."

"Maybe it's time you go to the gym and lift some weights or punch some bags," Jackson suggested.

"Maybe," Lee replied listlessly.

"Buddy, you've got to buck up," Jackson said. "This will all pass and you'll be just fine. A year from now you'll be living your best life."

Lee grinned at him. "That's why I wanted to have lunch with you today. I knew you would remind me that I'll be okay."

"You will be," Jackson replied firmly.

After lunch was over and the two men parted ways, Jackson returned home. He wished he would have made plans to see Josie that evening, but he hadn't.

Time seemed to move ridiculously slow over the next day, but finally it was time to meet Josie at Vincent's. When he pulled into the parking lot, she was there, looking gorgeous in a yellow dress that showed off her perfect figure. Her hair was loose…a black waterfall of richness that fell around her shoulders.

He got out of his car and she ran toward him, a smile on her lips that warmed him as if he'd swallowed the sun whole. "Hi, beautiful," he said.

"Hi, handsome," she replied.

He walked her to the passenger side of the car and opened the door. After she slid inside, he closed the door and then hurried around to the driver's door. He was excited to spend more time with her. He was looking forward to her seeing his home and excited to cook for her. He'd never felt this way before. Damn, he was definitely falling hard for her.

He got into the car and grinned at her. "You look absolutely gorgeous this evening."

"Thanks," she replied with a smile of her own.

"Are you hungry?"

"I'm definitely getting there," she replied.

"Then let's get you to my place where I've got a couple of filets mignons just waiting to be thrown on the grill." He started the car engine and headed out of Vincent's parking lot.

"I'm looking forward to you seeing my place tonight," he said.

"I'm looking forward to it, too," she replied.

"So, what's new with you since I last saw you?" he asked.

"The last time we saw each other and parted ways at the tree trunk, I was chased through the swamp by a man wearing a ski mask," she said.

Jackson slammed on his brakes, nearly coming to a full halt in the middle of the street as he shot her a horrified glance. "Are you joking with me right now? Please tell me you're joking."

"Trust me, it's no joke," she replied somberly.

"So…so…tell me more. God, Josie, I'm just glad you're here with me right now." He stepped on the gas once again after shooting a worried look at her.

"There isn't much more to tell," she replied. "He chased me and I managed to escape him. If he would have caught me, I carry a knife at all times for my protection."

"Do you carry it at your waist?" he asked.

"I do… How did you know?" she asked curiously.

He shot her another quick glance. "When we embraced the other night, I felt it and wondered what it was. Do you have any idea who it was who chased you?"

"Not a clue."

"Do…do you think it was the Honey Island Swamp Monster killer?" He reached out and took her hand in his. He held it tight, thinking of how frightened she must have been.

"It could have been, but I don't want to talk about all that right now."

"I'm just so glad you're here and that you weren't hurt," he replied.

She gently pulled her hand away from his. "Both hands on the steering wheel, *mon cher*. You're carrying precious cargo."

"I am, indeed," he replied. His fear for her still caused his heart to beat an accelerated tempo. Somebody in a ski mask had chased her? Who? Who could it have possibly been and what had he wanted with her? It could have only been something bad. Thank God, she had escaped.

He would honor her wishes not to talk about it anymore right now, but he couldn't promise he wouldn't talk to her about it later on.

It took only a few more minutes for him to pull into his driveway. His townhouse was one of four units. He'd bought into the condo style of living for simplicity. These units were high-end and here his lawn was mowed and the exterior of the building was kept up by the association. He'd lived here for eight years and still found it to be perfect for him.

"Come on in," he said as he opened the front door and allowed her to sweep past him. Once again, as she walked by him, he caught the scent of her, that heady fragrance that half-dizzied him.

As she walked into his living room and looked around, he followed her gaze. His black sofa was long and sleek, as was the matching side chair. The coffee and end tables were glass and silver and there was a nice built-in bar in one corner of the room.

He'd always been satisfied with his living conditions, but now as he looked around, he realized they were cold and sterile and without a hint of the person who lived here.

"Very nice," she said.

He laughed. "Don't lie. I just now realize that the place definitely needs a woman's touch. Please, have a seat." He gestured toward the sofa. "Would you like a drink?"

"If you have it, I wouldn't mind a cola with a splash of whiskey," she replied as she sank down on the sofa.

"Coming right up." He went over to the bar to prepare their drinks. He'd already made a salad and baked the potatoes so all he had to do was start up the grill on his patio and cook the steaks.

He made her drink and then one for himself and joined her on the sofa. "Now, tell me what you really think about my space."

She took a sip of her drink and then placed it on one of the coasters that were on the coffee table. "It's beautiful, but there's really nothing of you here. Didn't you tell me your favorite color was blue?"

"It is," he agreed, surprised that she'd even remembered that minute detail about him.

"Then why not bring some blue into this room?" she asked. "Maybe some pictures on the walls or some accents in blue?"

"Why don't you help me with decorating in here? I told you, it needs a woman's touch and I can't think of any other woman I'd want decorating it than you." He took a drink but kept his gaze solely focused on her.

"If you really wanted me to do something in here, I would be willing to help you. But, Jackson, don't change things in here on my account."

"I'm not, but I wouldn't mind some changes to make things a little brighter and homier. And speaking of that, why don't we take our drinks out to my patio and I'll put the steaks on." If he sat next to her on the sofa for too much longer, he'd want to pull her into his arms and forget all about dinner.

Tonight, he was really hoping that they would take their relationship to the next level and they'd make love. It began with dinner and hopefully it would end up in his bed.

Chapter Five

Dinner was absolutely delicious. The salad was crisp and refreshing and the potato was also good. The steak was cooked to perfection and she really enjoyed it all.

She and Jackson sat in his dining room to eat and, as always, their conversation flowed easily. He was interesting and funny and she really enjoyed the time she spent with him.

She kept having to remind herself that she was just using Jackson, because the truth of the matter was he was getting to her. As much as she hated to admit it, he was definitely getting into her heart.

She'd heard through the grapevine that Patricia Bardot was having one of her big galas next week-end, and she wondered if Jackson would invite her to go with him? Or was he actually like Gentry and would not want to be seen with her in such a huge public setting?

Having dinner with her at the café hadn't been a big social outing of the two of them together, nothing like the gala where everyone who was anyone would attend. The gala would be the perfect place to get the opportunity to identify her rapist. If she could just smell him again and hear his voice, then she'd know who it was. And she was fairly certain the man would be at the gala.

After dinner, she insisted she help with the kitchen cleanup and once that was done, they got fresh drinks and returned to the sofa in the living room.

"Dinner was absolutely delicious," she said once they were seated. "I loved the steak. It was so flavorful and juicy."

He grinned. "My next goal is to make you a good juicy cheeseburger."

She laughed. "You can try all you want, but a good piece of fish will always be my first choice."

"Ah, but you haven't tasted my cheeseburger yet." His eyes gleamed with the teasing light she loved.

"And you haven't tasted my grilled fish yet," she replied.

"I see some cook-offs coming in our future. And speaking of the future, I don't know if you've heard about it or not, but Mrs. Patty Bardot is having one of her big galas next Saturday night, and I was wondering if you'd be my date. I'd love to show you off to all my friends."

A warmth of feminine pleasure washed over her. It had nothing to do with the fact that she'd wanted this to catch her attacker. For just a moment, it was strictly the fact that he wanted her by his side and it was a place she wanted to be.

"I'd love to go with you," she replied.

"Great. And I'd be happy to buy you a dress to wear for the evening."

She stiffened and narrowed her eyes at him. "And I find the very idea of that highly offensive."

He instantly looked at her apologetically. "I'm sorry. I didn't mean to offend you. I just… I've often bought dresses for my dates in the past."

"I would never allow a man to pay for my clothes for a date out. I buy my own clothes and I assure you I will be appropriately dressed for the gala." She continued to pin him with her gaze, irritated that he would even think she would accept such a gift from him.

"Don't be angry with me, Josie. I forgot for a moment that you aren't like the other women I've dated in the past. Even though they came from money, they were always eager for me to buy them clothes, and if they could get a piece of jewelry from me, it was even better. I'm truly sorry that I would even believe for one minute that you were like them."

He looked so miserable she couldn't maintain any further anger toward him. He couldn't help it that, in this instance, he was nothing more than a creature of habit. She found it despicable that the women in his past had obviously taken advantage of his wealth and kindness.

"I accept your apology. But just remember, Jackson, I'm with you because I want to be, not because of anything I can get from you."

A warm smile lit his features. "I really like that about you."

She laughed. "And there are many things I like about you, too."

"I hope so," he replied, suddenly serious. "Because I'm more than a little bit crazy about you, Josie."

He leaned forward and she knew he wanted to kiss her. And she wanted his kiss. Oh, how she wanted it. She bent forward into him and his mouth took hers.

It began as a sweet, tender kiss, one that swelled a simmering heat inside her. Quickly, he deepened the kiss by swirling his tongue with hers. She welcomed it, leaning even closer to him.

The kiss went on until she was half-breathless and she finally pulled away from him. His eyes were filled with a wild hunger that shot a warm delicious shiver down her back.

"Josie… I… I want you," he said, his voice sounding deeper than usual. "I want you so badly."

"And I… I want you, too." It was true, the kiss had stirred up a wealth of desire inside her. She definitely wanted him, too.

He stood and held his hand out to her. "Josie, will you come with me to my bedroom?"

She hesitated only a moment and then stood and took his hand. Her heart raced with both excitement and a touch of anxiety as he led her down the hallway.

They passed what looked like a spare bedroom

with a queen bed decorated in blacks and yellows, then a bathroom decorated in the same colors.

Finally, he led her into a large bedroom with a king-size bed, a long dresser with a mirror and a small lamp illuminating the room from one of the nightstands.

The bed was covered in a navy spread that matched the curtains at the window. He immediately took her back in his arms and his mouth sought hers once again. She molded herself to him and he wrapped his arms tightly around her. The kiss deepened, but as he strengthened his grip on her, an unexpected flashback rushed through her brain.

A bag falling over her head…hands shoving her to the ground…her hands tied in front of her…and… she gasped and took a step back from Jackson. For a brief moment, she was trapped between the past and the present, caught between desire for Jackson and the horrible encounter with her assailant.

Jackson instantly dropped his arms to his sides. "Josie?" It was a tender inquiry and to her horror, she burst into tears.

"Hey, honey… Josie, what's going on? If you don't want to be with me, it's okay," he continued.

She shook her head as her tears continued to flow uncontrollably. She sank down on the edge of the bed and he sat beside her, leaving several inches between them.

"Josie, please talk to me. Tell me what's going on." His voice was soft and filled with a tenderness she hadn't realized she'd yearned for until this moment.

She cried for a few more minutes and then finally pulled herself together, although she couldn't look at him. "Almost ten months ago I was raped." The words fell from her with a new wave of tears seeping out of her eyes.

"Oh, Josie. Honey, I'm so sorry that happened to you." His voice held both a touch of outrage and a wealth of gentleness. "Can…can I just hold you right now?"

"I… I'd like that," she replied.

He wrapped his arm around her shoulders and pulled her into him. Weakly, she leaned into his strength, his warmth, and she was surprised as always that she felt so safe and secure there.

"Do you want to talk about it?" he asked softly.

She hadn't spoken to anyone about the assault since she'd talked to Chief of Police Gravois on the night that it had happened. There had been nobody to talk to about it. But now there was Jackson, sweet and kind Jackson.

"I'd just made a fish run into town and was coming back home," she began, fighting to keep her wild emotions in check. "I had only gone a few feet into the swamp when he came up behind me. Before I even knew he was there, he pulled a black bag over my head and tightened it around my neck. I… I thought he was going to strangle me to death, but then he shoved me hard and I fell to my hands and knees. He flipped me over to my back and managed to tie my wrists together and then…then he raped me."

The words fled from her in a rush, as if the faster she spoke them the less chance they had to hurt her. But the outrage of the violation, her anger over the injustice of it all, gripped her before the actual physical and emotional pain of the attack did. That let her know she was healing. But she still wanted justice for herself and anyone else the man had assaulted. Maybe he'd done it to other women who hadn't reported it.

"Josie, I'm so very sorry that happened to you. Honey, you definitely didn't deserve it," Jackson said. They were words she hadn't realized she needed to hear until this very moment.

"This makes me so damned angry for you," he continued. "Did you report this to the police?"

She nodded. "I spoke directly to Chief Gravois the moment I managed to untie myself, pulled myself together and could get to the police station."

Jackson's arm tightened around her. "And what did he do about it?"

A small bitter laugh escaped her. "Nothing. He made a report and told me he'd check it out, but as far as I know he did nothing except tell me I should be a lot more careful walking through the swamp alone."

Jackson released a string of curse words. "I swear, we've got to do something about that man. He's not worthy of his position." He drew in a deep breath and then released it audibly. "Do you have any idea who attacked you? Did you see anything that might have given you a clue to his identity?"

The last thing she wanted was for Jackson to somehow put it together that she was using him in the effort to identify her assailant. "I'm guessing it was one of the men from the swamp, but I don't know enough to specifically identify him."

"I can't say it enough, Josie. I'm so sorry for what you went through. Something like this should never ever happen to any woman."

"Thank you. I think one of the hardest parts was that I had nobody to talk to about it."

"Well, now you have me. Josie, anytime you feel the need to talk about it, anytime you need a reminder that you are important and this should have never happened to you, then you come directly to me," he said.

Her heart warmed with his words, with the way he was handling her with such kindness, such gentleness. A deep wave of guilt also flashed through her.

She looked up at him and offered him a half smile. "Poor Jackson, here you were expecting a night of wild romance and instead I give you all this."

"Honey, there will be many more opportunities for wild romance between us but only when you're sure you're ready." He kissed her on her forehead. "Now what do you say we go back into the living room and have another drink."

She nodded and together they got up from his bed and she went back to the sofa while he grabbed their glasses and returned to the bar. As she watched him making their drinks, a new wave of guilt swept through her. The guilt over using him was coupled with the surprising realization that she was falling for him. How had that happened and so quickly?

Still, no matter how much she cared for him, she told herself that she wasn't looking for a real relationship with him. There was no way she'd put her heart on the line to be hurt another time. She had to keep her heart carefully locked away from him.

"Have you heard of Mrs. Patty's galas before?" he asked once they each had a drink again and he was back on the sofa next to her.

"I've heard a few stories about them," she replied. "I've heard they are over-the-top with alcohol flowing and expensive tidbits being served and naked dancers on all of the tables."

He laughed. "You're definitely right in the first two descriptions, but I have yet to see anyone dancing naked on the tables. However, for the last gala Mrs. Patty flew in thousands of different types of butterflies and had them released all at the same time."

"Now that's a woman who has way too much money," she observed.

"You're right. She was quite wealthy on her own and then she married Harry Bardo who was a multimillionaire. When he died, he left her everything. She now has more money than she could ever spend in five lifetimes. She's definitely the richest woman in Black Bayou."

"I hope she's donating some of that money to charity," Josie said.

"I know one of her pet projects is a dog rescue. She has events specifically to raise money for it. I've heard she also donates heavily for breast cancer."

"Well, that's good to hear."

"And I'll tell you something else about the upcoming gala." He grinned at her and his eyes sparkled brightly. "I can't wait to walk in with you on my arm."

"That's what makes you different from the last man I dated," she replied.

He raised an eyebrow. "Want to tell me about your past relationship? Or maybe you find it too personal to talk about with me."

She laughed. "I'd say I've already talked about some pretty personal things so one more thing won't matter now. Besides, I'm the one who brought it up. You might know him, Gentry O'Connal?"

Jackson frowned. "Yeah, I know him. So, you dated him?"

"I did. I don't remember why he was around the swamp in the first place, but I ran into him one evening when I was on my way to Vincent's for a few groceries. He was very nice and flirtatious and he asked me if he could meet me the next day. Anyway, we dated for almost six months but we always spent our time together at my place."

She shifted her position on the sofa and quickly took a sip of her drink, and then continued. "I finally asked him if we could go to the café to eat or someplace else besides my shanty and that's when he told me what he really thought about me. He said he enjoyed spending time with me, but I was a swamp woman and he had no interest in pursuing anything deep with me or being seen in public with me. That's when I realized I was nothing more to him than a dirty little secret and that was also the last time I saw him."

"I've never liked him and I definitely like him even less now," Jackson replied. "As far as I'm concerned, I have always found him to be an arrogant jerk." His gaze held hers. "Were you in love with him?"

She thought about it for several seconds. "I thought I was in love with him at the time, but looking back I think I was just lonely and this all happened immediately after my parents were both gone. He momentarily took the pain of their loss away and soothed some of my loneliness."

He reached out and took her hand in his. "I'll tell you this, Josie, you deserve far better than a man like Gentry. I can't imagine not wanting to take you out and show you off. I want my friends to not only see how beautiful you are, but also how bright and intelligent you are, too. When I look at you, I don't think swamp and when I think about myself, I don't think town. I think of us as two people with different backgrounds who are enjoying each other's company."

She squeezed his hand. "I don't know how I got so lucky to meet you, Jackson."

"I feel the same way about you. I had just about

given up on finding a woman who would touch me on all the levels that you do," he replied.

She gently pulled her hand away from his. "I think on that note, I'd like to go home. This has definitely been an evening of crazy emotions for me and I'm exhausted."

The truth of the matter was she wanted to stop him before he said anything else about the way he felt toward her. Although she loved hearing it, at the same time she didn't want to hear it. She had to remember what she was doing with him.

"Of course," he said and stood from the sofa.

"I'm sorry if this evening didn't work out as we thought it was going to," she said as she also got up.

"Josie, please don't apologize. I'm glad we're at a place where you felt you could trust me with everything you told me." He grabbed his keys from the end table and together they left out his front door.

Darkness had fallen and as she slid into the passenger side of the car, she realized she really was mentally and emotionally exhausted. Talking about the rape had been extremely difficult for her, but she was glad she'd shared that traumatic event with Jackson. She'd been surprised how much his kindness and words of support had touched her heart. He was getting in so deep…too deep. Somehow, she needed to slow things down with him.

When she'd seen the opportunity to use him, she'd never expected to like him so much. The best thing that could happen would be that she identified her attacker at the gala and then she would break things off with Jackson and never see him again.

That way he wouldn't have a chance to break her heart, because if she continued seeing him, she believed that eventually, just like Gentry, he would break her heart.

THEY WERE BOTH silent on the ride home. It wasn't an awkward silence, but rather a companionable one. He glanced over to her several times as he drove, wanting to assure himself that she was okay.

The thought that she'd been raped burned in his very soul. He'd love to meet the man who had assaulted her and beat his face in. When he thought of her fear…her violation in that moment, it made him so angry he couldn't see straight.

The fact that Gravois hadn't taken the crime seriously only fueled his anger to a higher level. The man was utterly useless and maybe it was time to lead some sort of a recall effort and get him out of office once and for all.

He finally pulled up in Vincent's parking lot and stopped his engine. "I'll walk you in to your place," he said.

"Don't be ridiculous," she replied with a small laugh. "You'd get lost and then I won't have a date for the gala."

"Surely, I'd find my way out in a week," he protested with a laugh of his own.

"I don't know. There are legends about townies who

entered the swamp and got lost for years. They wander the wild half mad and howl at the moon at night."

"You just made that up," he accused her.

She grinned. "Busted. Still, there's no way I want you to walk me home. Seriously, Jackson, I'll be fine. I have my knife and I can find hiding places in the swamp that most people wouldn't even know about." She reached out and touched the back of his hand. "Please, don't worry about me."

"I can't help but worry about you," he replied. "It was just a few nights ago that somebody chased you through the swamp."

"But he didn't catch me. Now, it's time to say goodnight." She opened the car door and got out and he did the same. They reached each other at the front of the car.

"Josie, can I give you a hug?" he asked, sensitive to what she might or might not want or need from him right now.

"I'm hoping you're going to give me a big hug and a kiss," she replied.

He pulled her into his arms and she immediately leaned into him. "Oh, God, Josie, I wish I could magically take away all your pain," he whispered into her ear. "I wish I could take away any bad memories that you have and replace them with wonderful ones."

"You're definitely helping," she replied. She looked up at him and her dark gray eyes shone silver in the moonlight. "Please, kiss me, Jackson."

She didn't have to ask him twice. He covered her

mouth with his in a tender kiss that he hoped reached in and soothed all the rough edges her past had created in her. She'd been through so much and yet had survived it all with strength and dignity. He admired her so much for that.

The kiss lasted only a moment and then he released her and she stepped back from him. "Will I see you tomorrow?" he asked.

"I could meet you at the tree trunk," she replied. "Whatever time works for you."

"Why don't I bring lunch and we can have a picnic there," he suggested.

"Oh, that sounds like fun. Then we'll meet around noon?"

"Bring your appetite," he replied.

"I will. Good night, Jackson."

"'Night Josie." He watched until she disappeared from sight, swallowed up by the swamp that had created her. He hoped she made it home okay but he couldn't help but worry.

There was a murderer loose who had the women in the swamp in his sights. Was that who had chased Josie a few nights before? Had it been the killer dubbed the Honey Island Swamp Monster?

He turned and got back into his car, his head filled with all the things Josie had shared with him tonight. She had definitely been through a lot, but he was amazed and awed by her strength and resilience.

She was exactly the kind of woman he'd always dreamed of for himself. He'd wanted a strong, independent woman who was formidable in her beliefs and convictions, a woman who would both challenge and delight him.

He'd given up on finding that woman. He'd dated a lot before Josie, but he found most of the women he dated were either after his money or simpering women who agreed with everything he said.

Josie was exactly what he wanted and he hoped she wanted him, too. He definitely wanted to help her get over her past traumas. Right now, he just hoped she got home safely and would meet him the next day for lunch.

He was far too wired up to just go home and go to bed. It wasn't that late, so he headed for Tremont's for a drink before returning home.

On a Friday night, the place was hopping. The dining room was full and half a dozen men sat at the long polished bar. He immediately spied Brian at the end of the bar with Sonny sitting next to him.

"Gentlemen," he greeted them.

"Hey, man," Brian said.

"Am I intruding?" Jackson asked.

"Hell no, grab a stool and join us," Sonny said. "We're just sitting here bitching and moaning about life."

Jackson sank down on the stool next to Sonny. "Are we bitching and moaning about anything in particular?"

"Nah, just life in general," Brian replied.

"How are Cynthia and the kids doing?" Jackson asked Brian.

"They're all good. It's the stock market that's driving me crazy right now."

"Ha, that's driving everyone crazy right now," Jackson replied. "One day it's up and the next day it's down."

Jackson ordered his drink and for the next half an hour he and his buddies talked about business, Sonny's latest dating escapades and Brian's kids.

"What would you all think about starting a recall effort on Gravois to get him out of office?" Jackson asked.

"I'd be in," Sonny said. "But do you have any idea what is involved in trying to do something like that?"

"No, but I intend to research it to find out," Jackson replied. "He's inept and lazy, among other things. I wonder how many other people in town have lost faith in law enforcement because of him?"

"I wonder how many people have just stopped reporting crimes because they know nothing will be done about them," Sonny said.

"That's definitely a horrible thought," Jackson replied.

"I think you have to start a petition and get so many signatures on it to start," Brian said.

"So, if I get this thing started, will you both help me get the signatures that are required?" Jackson asked.

They both said they would be in to help and by that time Jackson was ready to call it a night. He said his goodbyes and then walked out of the restaurant and into the sultry night air.

The rest of the week flew by quickly. His picnic lunch with Josie was lighthearted and fun and he saw her two more days during the week, one day for more fishing and another when he took her to his parents' house for dinner.

By the end of the evening, his parents positively adored her. Jackson was at an age where his parents didn't care who he fell in love with, they just wanted him happy in love. His mother definitely wanted to see him get married as she was looking forward to having grandchildren as soon as possible.

Finally, the evening of the gala arrived. As he dressed for the night, excited energy raced through him. He couldn't wait to see Josie. He couldn't wait to spend hours at the gala with her by his side.

Mrs. Patty's galas warranted formal attire so Jackson was wearing his navy tuxedo. He had no idea what Josie was wearing. She had refused to even tell him the color of her gown. Whatever she wore, he knew she would look absolutely stunning.

Finally, it was time for him to leave to pick her up. As usual, he was meeting her in Vincent's parking lot. As he left his place, he was grateful that the weather was perfect. The skies were clear and it was a little cooler than it had been, making it a perfect night for a party. He knew from past parties that much of the gala would take place on the patio and in the vast gardens in Mrs. Patty's huge backyard.

As he drove toward Vincent's, a new burst of excitement danced inside him. He was eager for his friends to meet Josie. He knew without a doubt she would charm them all. Even Lee, who hated all women right now, would be unable to find fault with sweet, wonderful Josie.

It was important to him that his friends like her. In the future, there would be times where they would all be together both for social events or just hanging out and having beers and conversation with each other. She would fit right in with all of them.

He saw her the moment he turned into the parking lot. She was an absolute vision in a one-shoulder gown that fell in a column of coral silk to her feet.

He thought his breath might have stopped for a moment as he took in her beauty. Her hair was twisted up, but the beauty of the darkness against the color of the gown stole his breath away. She looked like a Greek goddess.

As she smiled at him, a burst of warmth shot throughout his entire body and he knew in that moment that he was definitely madly in love with her.

Chapter Six

Josie carried with her a plastic bag containing the jeans, blouse and shoes she had worn to leave the swamp. She had dressed for the gala in Vincent's ladies' room. Thankfully, Vincent always kept the restrooms pristine.

She'd been ridiculously nervous about how she looked, but as Jackson got out of his car to greet her, she knew by his smile and the heat in his eyes that she looked okay.

"Josie, you are positively stunning," he said in greeting.

"Thank you, and you look very nice, too." He looked better than nice in the navy tuxedo that fit him perfectly and brought out the bright blue of his eyes.

He opened the car door for her. "Let me get you inside quickly before another man comes along and steals you right away from me," he said.

She laughed. "You don't have to worry about another man stealing me away from you, Jackson." She slid into the car. "I always go home with the man I come with."

"Aside from looking gorgeous, are you ready for this big gala?" he asked once he joined her in the car.

"I've had nervous butterflies darting around in my stomach for most of the afternoon," she confessed. "And right now, they are definitely flying around fast and furiously."

"Don't worry, you'll be just fine," he assured her.

"Just make me one promise."

"And what's that?" he asked curiously.

"Promise me you won't leave my side. I won't know a soul there except for you."

"That's an easy promise to make," he replied with a smile. "When you're with the prettiest woman in the place, you don't ever want to leave her side." He flashed her another smile that warmed her from head to toe, then he started the car and they took off.

She couldn't help but be super nervous. She would be spending the evening with people she didn't know, many of them who shunned anything and anyone from the swamp.

However, she would do anything possible to find the man who had raped her. There was no question in her mind that he would probably be there tonight. This night could possibly be the beginning of the end of her time with Jackson.

That thought shot an unexpected piercing pain through her heart. She already felt incredibly guilty for using him, particularly since she'd had dinner with his parents. They had been lovely and welcoming, and Josie had felt like she was there under false pretenses.

In the end, she knew there would be no love story between her and Jackson. They were from two different worlds and she would never truly trust a town man again with her heart.

She shoved these thoughts out of her head as she once again focused on what her mission was for the night. As Jackson flashed her a heated gaze, she realized despite her desire to the contrary, Jackson had managed to get into her heart. That would make her telling him goodbye all the more difficult.

She sat up straighter in her seat as they approached Mrs. Patty's home. It was a massive white two-story with six huge columns in the front. It was easily the biggest house in the town. The driveway was a circle and as vehicles pulled up, several valets in uniform helped the ladies out and then took the keys from the men and parked the cars in the side yard.

There was already a line of vehicles in front of them. "Looks like it's going to be a full house tonight," Jackson said.

"I certainly didn't expect a valet service to park the cars," she replied.

"Mrs. Patty definitely likes to do things right," he said.

She watched as ladies in lovely gowns and men in tuxedos got out of the cars and strolled up the long walkway to the front door.

Then it was their turn. Jackson got out of the car

and handed his keys to the attendant, but instead of allowing one of the uniformed men to help her out of the car, he hurried around the car and opened her door.

For just a moment, she wanted to tell him to get back in the car as quickly as possible and drive away. She couldn't do this. Her nerves pulsed through her entire body as she thought about the night to come.

"Josie?" He held out a hand to her. She mentally shook herself. She had a mission tonight. This might be the very best chance for her to catch her predator. She grasped his hand firmly and got out of the car. Once she was out, he grasped her elbow firmly. "Are you okay?" he asked.

"I'm fine…just ridiculously nervous," she admitted.

He squeezed her elbow and flashed her a bright smile. "Don't worry, Josie, I told you that you're going to be just fine," he repeated to her. "Just be yourself."

The moment they walked through the double doors, she wasn't fine; she was completely overwhelmed. The foyer was large, with high ceilings and an ornate round table holding a colorful flower arrangement that was huge. Couples mingled all around, some with drinks in hand and others without.

Music played overhead and the sound of laughter and chatter filled the air. Jackson took her hand and led her through the foyer and into an enormous living room. There were only a few people standing and talking together in here.

Ahead, she saw where the real party was. Wide glass doors opened out to the night. "Before we do anything else, we need to pay our respects to Mrs. Patty," Jackson said as he guided her toward the open doors.

They walked outside into a piazza-like area with silver flagstones under their feet and low lights shining from several tall attractive light fixtures. The air was sweetly scented with all the flowers that lined the various pathways that wound through the lawn.

People stood around, laughing and talking in small groups as uniformed waitstaff offered hors d'oeuvres and drinks from silver trays.

There were a lot of men there with wives or dates. How awkward would it be for her to ask if she could smell them and hear them talk? Of course, that would be ridiculous, but hopefully by the end of the night Jackson would have introduced her to most of them and at least she would be able to hear them speak. She knew that was the way she was going to definitely identify her monster.

Mrs. Patty sat in an oversize white wicker chair on one side of the festivities. Josie would guess the woman was in her mid-eighties. Her snow-white hair was pulled up into an attractive twist, exposing her elegant long neck and the sparkling blue earrings that hung from her ears.

She was a slender woman and her blue gown showcased her bright blue eyes. Although her features were all soft, an aura of steely power radiated out from her. It was obvious that she was holding court from her chair.

"Good evening, Mrs. Patty," Jackson said. "Thank you so much for inviting me to this evening's festivities."

"Jackson, you know the only reason I invite you here is because I like eye candy," she replied. "Now, introduce me to this lovely lady by your side."

"This is Josie Cadieux," he said.

"Josie." Mrs. Patty held out a hand and Josie took it with hers. "You are a beautiful woman, but are you also a smart woman?"

"I like to think I am," Josie replied.

"Then what are you doing here with Jackson?"

Josie smiled at the older woman. "I like eye candy, too."

Mrs. Patty stared at her for a moment and then laughed. She gave Josie's hand a squeeze and then released it. "Go, get yourself drinks and some food and enjoy yourselves." She shooed them away.

"She likes you," Jackson said as they moved away from the older woman.

"How do you know?" Josie asked.

"She likes people who make her laugh."

"Then I feel like I just passed a huge test," she replied.

He laughed and grabbed her hand. "You did, and now let's get a drink and then mingle."

And mingle they did. Jackson seemed to know everyone and she was introduced to tons of people within the first hour. She listened carefully to each man she met, but none of them had the particular voice she sought.

The scents that filled the air was a combination of garden flowers, booze and the various perfumes and colognes that everyone wore. It was impossible to pick out the man who wore the particular scent she remembered from that horrible night.

It was about that time when he introduced her to Andrew Bailey and his girlfriend, Belinda. "Hey, I've been looking all over for Brian and Sonny and Lee. Have you seen any of them around here tonight?"

"No, but Sonny told me they weren't going to make it tonight because the three of them were heading to Florida this morning to check out some piece of real estate that Brian is interested in buying."

"Oh, it must have been planned in a hurry because none of them mentioned anything about it to me," Jackson replied.

"I don't know about when they planned it, but I got the definite impression it was a spur-of-the-moment thing. I just had a quick phone call with Sonny this morning and he mentioned they'd be missing tonight because of the trip," Andrew replied.

"I guess I'll just catch up with them all when they get back in town," Jackson replied.

"Well, that's a bit disappointing," he said as they walked away from Andrew. "I was really hoping you'd meet my close friends tonight."

"There will be another time," she replied.

He continued to introduce Josie to more people as the evening continued. She sipped on a fruity drink and also enjoyed the food that was offered, little tidbits that popped with flavor. There were crackers with cream cheese and caviar, lobster bites on puffed pastry and dozens of other delicious items.

For the most part, she found everyone pleasant and welcoming, but there was a group of women gathered around the bar and at one point she caught tidbits of their conversation. They apparently had imbibed in more than a few drinks and were unaware of how loud they were talking.

"I just can't imagine what Jackson is doing with her," a short blonde said.

"Oh, I can certainly imagine. You know those swamp women have no morals at all," another tall brunette woman said. "Who knows what she's doing under the sheets with him, if you know what I mean."

"When I was younger, her mother used to clean for us. She was one of the laziest women we'd ever had and we had to fire her after a couple of weeks," a third woman said with a mean laugh.

Josie tightened her hands into fists as a rich anger swept through her. She knew the woman who had spoken. Her name was Allison Ingraham and Josie's mother had quit that job because the Ingraham house was a filthy big hoard.

Jackson, who was visiting with one of his friends, wasn't aware of the women talking and despite Josie's anger over the mischaracterization of her hardworking mother, she did nothing.

The last thing she wanted to do was cause a scene and to what end? She knew there were probably a lot of people here tonight who didn't believe she belonged among them, who saw her as trash. She'd seen the surprised looks and had been aware of the whispers that had occurred as they passed various people.

The real disappointment of tonight was that she felt as if she'd met nearly every man at the gala and most of the men who lived in town and none of their voices identified one of them as her attacker.

The night ended with an explosion of fireworks. As the fiery colorful show filled the sky, Jackson pulled her into his arms and gave her a tender kiss.

The feel of his lips against hers moved the explosions from the sky to the very pit of her stomach. She was definitely more than a little bit crazy about Jackson.

"I'm still disappointed that you didn't get to meet my buddies tonight," he said once they were in his car and headed back to Vincent's.

"Surely, there will be another chance for me to meet them," she replied.

"For sure. I can't wait to show you off to them." He cast her a quick glance and smile. "I was so happy and so proud to be with you tonight. Did you have a good time?"

"I had a very good time," she replied. "Everyone was very nice, the food was delicious and my date was wonderfully attentive and charming."

"That's nice to hear. From my take, my date was not only the most beautiful woman at the party, but you were also gracious and welcoming to everyone. Seriously, Josie, I was so proud to have you by my side."

"Oh, Jackson, you're making me blush."

He laughed. "I love your blushes. You were also the most intelligent woman at the gala."

"And what makes you think that?" she asked.

"Well, you were there with me, so that shows me how very intelligent you are to pick me as your date."

It was her turn to laugh. "I hate to burst your bubble, but you were my only option as a date."

"Then I guess that makes me one lucky guy," he replied.

By that time, they had arrived in Vincent's parking lot. Jackson cut the engine, she turned and grabbed her bag of clothing from the back seat and then together they got out of the car.

"Thank you, Jackson, for inviting me tonight," she said. "I really had a wonderful time."

"Whoa, I'm not going anywhere yet. Go change your clothes and I'll wait here for you." He leaned against the car and so she hurried to the restroom to change back into the clothes that were in the bag.

She exchanged the elegant gown for a T-shirt and jeans, and her pretty high heels for tennis shoes. She paused for a moment and stared at her reflection in the warped mirror over the sink.

She'd gone into all this with Jackson in order to

use him to find her rapist. She'd never intended to develop any real feelings for him.

But she had, and now she didn't know what to do. She'd sworn after Gentry she would never ever date a town man again. In fact, after her rape she'd decided that she would live the rest of her life alone. She'd made an exception with Jackson because she'd been on a mission.

She needed to break things off with him…before she fell more deeply in love with him. She would never believe there was a future with him.

However, there were still some of his friends she hadn't met yet. Was it possible one of his close buddies was the guilty man? For Jackson's sake, she certainly hoped not, but she couldn't be sure until she met them.

No, she couldn't stop yet. She at least had to meet his friends. She'd give it another week or so and if she hadn't found her assailant by then, then it would be time to let Jackson go. Both for his sake and for hers.

IT WAS ON Wednesday when Jackson finally heard from his buddies and they all planned to meet for lunch at Tremont's. As he drove to the restaurant, as always Josie was on his mind.

He'd never felt this kind of love for a woman before. Josie had stirred a depth of feeling inside him he'd never had before. Each time he was with her, his love for her only deepened. Each time he was with her, he dreaded the time when he had to tell her goodbye for the day.

However, he had no real clue what she felt for him. Oh, he knew she liked him and apparently enjoyed spending time with him. When he kissed her, she responded to him with the same fire that he had, but was she really falling in love with him?

He desperately hoped so. He wanted to marry her. He was ready to start planning a real future with her. He knew already that he wanted to spend the rest of his life with her. But maybe things were moving a little too fast for her.

He wanted to tell her how he felt, but he also didn't want to scare her away if she needed more time. There was no question that his feelings for her had developed very quickly.

He shoved these thoughts out of his mind as he pulled into a parking space in front of the restaurant. When he went inside, Lee and Sonny were already seated at a table.

"Ah, the vagabonds have finally returned," he said to them as he joined them.

"We got back in town late last night," Sonny replied.

"Is Brian joining us?" Jackson asked.

"Yeah, he called a few minutes ago and said he's running a little late, but he'll definitely be here," Lee said.

"He probably had a bunch of honey-dos this morning after being gone for a couple of days," Sonny said with a laugh.

"So, how was your trip? I was surprised when I

heard at the gala that you had all gone out of town," Jackson said.

"It was kind of a last-minute thing. A hotel that Brian had his eye on went up for sale and he wanted to get down to Florida, check it out and make an offer," Lee explained.

"And here's the man of the hour now," Sonny said as Brian approached their table.

He took the last seat at the table. "Hey, guys. Sorry I'm late."

"No problem," Jackson said. "They were just starting to fill me in on your trip. So, did you buy it?"

"Nah, once I got a closer look at the property, I realized it was going to cost a ton to renovate it and the owners weren't willing to budge at all on their price point, which was too damned high to start with. So, in the end I walked away from it."

"So, what took you all so long to come home?" Jackson asked.

"I twisted their arms into staying and enjoying a little mini-vacation. Our hotel was right on the water so we did some surfing and other water sports before coming back," Lee said.

"We also drank more than a little bit and hung out in the awesome bar right there in the hotel," Sonny added.

"But for God's sake, don't tell Cynthia any of that. As far as she is concerned, this trip was strictly business," Brian said.

"Well, you all missed a great gala," Jackson said.

"Needless to say, I wasn't going to go anyway," Lee said mournfully. "It's no fun to go places like that solo."

"But I knew you would be going with your new squeeze and that's why I didn't invite you on our little trip," Brian explained.

"My *new squeeze* was definitely the most beautiful woman at the party," Jackson replied. "She was charming and gracious and we both had a wonderful time."

"You sound like a man in love," Brian said.

"I am," Jackson admitted.

"I can't believe it took a swamp woman to get you out of the dating market," Lee said.

"I wish you all would stop referring to her that way," Jackson said in frustration. "Her name is Josie, not swamp woman." He was about to say more but at that moment the waitress appeared by the side of the table to take their orders.

While they ate, the topic of conversation changed to the usual things, business and Lee's divorce. Jackson was half grateful that the talk wasn't about him and Josie.

On the one hand, he wanted to shout out his love for her to the world, but on the other hand it felt good just to keep it to himself with these three men who seemed to only refer to her as Josie from the swamp. Dammit, why couldn't she just be Josie?

He only brought her up when they were almost finished with their meals. "Since you guys haven't had a chance to meet Josie yet, I'd like to invite you all to my place this Friday night for drinks. Brian, bring your wife and, Sonny, bring whoever you're dating. Lee, bring your sorrows and we'll help you drink them away."

Lee laughed. "There isn't enough booze in the world to take my sorrows away, but I'll be there."

"And I'll make sure to get a babysitter so we can be there," Brian said.

"I can't wait to meet the woman who has taken you off the dating market, so I'll definitely be there, too," Sonny added.

"Great, it should be a good night," Jackson said, pleased by the prospect of them all getting to know Josie. "It will be just drinks and some crackers and cheese and some laughs."

"Jackson, you seem to be moving pretty fast with this Josie," Lee said. "I would just suggest you take things slow with her. Don't jump into anything too quickly." He laughed. "Look at me, the man who is getting divorced is giving relationship advice."

Jackson laughed. "Things have been moving pretty quickly between us," he admitted. "But we've spent a lot of time together in a short period of time. I can't help the way I feel about her."

It was just after two o'clock when the men parted ways and Jackson headed home. He was looking forward to getting everyone together on Friday night. Those three men were his closest friends and it was important to him that they all get to know the woman he intended to have in his life for a very long time to come. He was sure Josie would charm them all with her quick wit and intelligence.

He was meeting her at their tree trunk in a couple of hours and he hoped she was in for Friday night. Their tree trunk… It was funny that he claimed a fallen dead tree trunk as theirs alone. But that place had become so important to him. It was close to where they had met and they had spent many hours there since then just talking about anything and everything.

Their conversations made him believe he knew her better than he had ever known a woman and he had laid open his life to her. The one thing they hadn't talked about was their feelings for each other, but that would come in due time. He wasn't going to be able to hold his feelings for her in for very much longer.

That night she took him to her place where she made him grilled fish and fried potatoes for dinner. As always, their conversation was light and easy through the meal.

After dinner and cleanup, they were seated on the sofa when he told her about the plans for Friday night. "That sounds like fun," she said. "I can't wait to finally meet your friends."

"And I can't wait for them to meet you," he replied.

"Tell me more about them." She leaned closer to him and a lick of hot desire shot off inside him.

He tried to tamp it down. "First there's Brian. He's

married to Cynthia who was his high school sweetheart and they have a boy and a girl. When we were young and running wild on the streets, he was usually the voice of reason."

"So, he's the one who kept you hooligans out of jail," she replied teasingly.

"Exactly. Then there's Lee. He's going through an acrimonious divorce right now. He's always been more than a little bit dramatic. He's the type that if he gets a cut on his finger, he assumes it's going to get infected and he's going to die. Right now, he's going through the world's worst divorce." Jackson frowned. "The only thing that worries me about him right now is how angry he's become with the divorce."

"Do you think he might go after his wife in some sort of a physical kind of way?" she asked.

"I would certainly hope not. I really can't imagine him doing anything like that. He's never shown any signs of being capable of hurting anyone."

"Well, that's good." She shifted positions and her scent eddied in the air all around him, re-stirring the lust inside him.

"Finally, there's Sonny. He's the quieter one of the bunch. He's just an all-round nice guy. He's single and still looking for his forever woman. Anyway, I'm eager for them to meet you."

"And I'm eager to meet them since they all mean so much to you," she replied.

It wasn't long after that when he decided it was time for him to leave her place. For some reason, tonight he was having trouble keeping his desire for her in check and the last thing he wanted to do was do something to offend her in any way.

He knew with her history he had to take things very slow with her physically and he was more than willing to do that for he was certain she was more than worth the wait. When it came to his physical desire for her, he just needed to take his cues from her.

She walked him to the tree trunk. “Will I see you again tomorrow?” he asked.

“No, tomorrow I’ll be busy checking lines and then tomorrow evening I’m going to take a load of fish into town. But I’ll be ready for you on Friday if you’re picking me up. Or I could drive to your place.”

“I’ll pick you up,” he replied. “The gang is going to be at my place around seven, so why don’t I pick you up around six? That will give us some time to visit before they all get there.”

The moonlight overhead stroked the beautiful planes of her face as she smiled at him. “Then I’ll be ready at six on Friday night.”

“Great. Can I kiss you good-night?”

Her smile grew brighter. “I’d like that.”

She leaned into him and he wrapped his arms around her. She fit so neat against him, as if she’d been made especially for him. The kiss began as something soft and tender, and then quickly escalated to something a bit more wild and hungry.

The earthy smell of the swamp coupled with her fresh slightly mysterious scent dizzied his senses. He felt half drugged by the heat, the place and the woman in his arms.

The kiss continued for only a short period of time and then he pulled away from her. “Oh, Josie. I want you so badly,” he said with a deep sigh.

“And I want you,” she replied softly. “Maybe on Friday night after your guests leave, we can have the romantic night we tried to have before.”

“Only if you’re ready for that,” he said. “I certainly don’t want to pressure you in any way.”

“I’m ready, Jackson.” Her eyes shone brightly as she looked up at him. “I really believe I’m ready.”

His heart swelled as he saw what appeared to be raw desire shining from her beautiful eyes. “We’ll play it by ear,” he finally said. “In the meantime, I’ll see you at six on Friday night.”

“Okay. Good night, Jackson.”

“’Night, Josie.”

He got back in his car and drew in several deep long breaths. He’d been looking forward to Josie meeting his friends on Friday night but now he had something else to look forward to. That was the night that they hopefully would take their relationship to the next level.

Chapter Seven

The next morning Josie decided to sit and fish for a while before she ran her lines. It had taken her a long time to go to sleep the night before and the thoughts that had kept sleep at bay still plagued her this morning.

She was so confused about Jackson. She believed she was in love with him and she'd never wanted that to happen. Last night when he'd kissed her good-night, she had wanted him more than she ever had. She wanted to be in his bed and feel his naked body against her own. She'd wanted him to kiss her until she was utterly mindless.

Without a doubt, he would be a tender, giving lover. She knew he'd take his lead from her and that only made her want him more. Would he make love to her and then go back to dating the kind of woman who would be more appropriate as a wife for him? She didn't believe so. She didn't believe she was just a conquest to win for him. But she just couldn't be sure. And that lingering doubt continued to confuse her.

She jumped up as she felt a bite on her line. She tipped the end of her pole to give it a little jerk and then began to reel in. The fish on the line felt big and feisty and when she finally got it in, it was a huge catfish.

"Now that's a fine catch." The familiar voice came out of the foliage next to her and half scared the hell out of her.

"Dammit, Gator, how did you manage to sneak up on me?" she said as the old man stepped out of the nearby brush and into her view.

He grinned at her. "You was busy landing that big fish and I was just creeping quietly."

"So, how's life treating you?" she asked as she took her hook out of the catfish's mouth and put the fish into a basket in the water.

"Not too bad. Mind if I sit with you for a spell?" he asked.

"Not at all. You know I always welcome your company," she replied.

He set down the walking stick he always carried with him and then eased himself to the ground. He was quiet as she rebaited her hook and cast the line out into the water. "How's life treating you?" he then asked.

As usual, the old man was clad in an old T-shirt, baggy jeans and alligator boots. The boots were made from the same alligator that had taken off three of his fingers.

"I can't complain," she replied. She returned to her seat on the bank.

"You seem to be spending a lot of time with that Jackson Fortier."

"I have been," she replied. "You been spying on me, Gator?" she asked teasingly.

He laughed and his dark eyes sparkled merrily. "You know I like walking about and on more than one occasion I've seen the two of you together. I keep my eyes and ears open around here, but I'd never spy on anyone."

"You ever been in love, Gator?" she asked. In all the years she had known the old man, he had always been alone.

"Oh, a million years ago I fell in love with a girl who was a neighbor of my ma and pa." He stared out across the water where the morning sun glittered gold. "Her name was Rosa and she was the prettiest, the sweetest woman in all of the swamp. Unfortunately, her and my baby boy died in childbirth."

"Oh, Gator, I'm so sorry," Josie said. "And you never found anyone else after her?"

Gator looked at her and all his features crinkled up in a smile. "Nah. I never wanted anyone else after that. After all these years, the memories of Rosa and her love still burns in my heart. Besides, I've become a strange old man who now feels married to the swamp and the gators I catch."

Josie returned his smile and then jumped up as she had another fish on her line. For the next twenty minutes or so, she and Gator small-talked while she caught three more fish.

"They're definitely biting good today," Gator said.

"They are, but I'm about done here. I still need to run my lines."

"Back to Jackson…you see a future with the city slicker?" Gator asked as he rose to his feet.

"Maybe," she replied. "I don't know for sure." There was no way to describe to Gator how confused she was about the man. Her love for him also battled with the fact that she'd been using him all along. Then there was her fear that she was from the swamp and would never be right for Jackson.

"And how do you think that would work out?" Gator looked at her and in the depths of his dark eyes, she saw age-old wisdom. "You got the swamp deep in your blood, Josie."

"I know that, but Peyton was a town woman and Beau was from the swamp. They've made it work between them," she replied.

"But Peyton ran the swamp as a young girl. She loved Beau, but she also loved the swamp as well. Jackson doesn't have the same ease around here."

He leaned down and picked up his walking stick and when he straightened, he smiled once again. "I just don't want to see you get hurt, Josie. I had great respect for your parents and I guess I just want you to be careful with your heart."

He cleared his throat as if not used to talking about such things of the heart. "And now I'll just take my leave." Without saying anything more, he turned, walked away and quickly disappeared back into the brush.

Josie packed up her fishing supplies. She felt as if the world had gone a little mad. She'd never seen the softer side of Gator before today.

Normally, he was just a tough old man who wandered the swamp and hunted for alligators. She never even noticed his missing three fingers as he managed to function as well as any ten-fingered person. And now he was giving her relationship advice… Definitely a little wild.

The morning passed quickly as she ran her lines and then took all her fish back to her place and put them in the big basket in the water. She had quite a haul to take into town later in the day.

She was looking forward to meeting Jackson's friends and she was desperately hoping she didn't recognize any of their voices. She would hate to find out that one of Jackson's closest friends was her attacker. It would break his heart.

Gator's words floated around in her head throughout the afternoon. He was right that the swamp was deep in her blood. She couldn't imagine living anyplace else. And she also knew that the swamp was definitely not in Jackson's blood.

In the depths of her heart, she still didn't believe there was a future with Jackson. After Friday night, it was time for her to part ways with him. It would break her heart more than a little bit, but better hurt now than when she was in any deeper with him.

She'd met men at the café with him and then a lot more men at the gala. She now didn't believe that she would be able to identify her attacker through him unless it was one of his friends. But really, what were the odds of that? So, it was time…past time to tell him goodbye.

The afternoon had turned cloudy and gray and when she loaded the fish in her old pickup, it was just after seven o'clock and dark with a false twilight.

She didn't want to think about Jackson anymore tonight. She just needed to focus on the job at hand and not anticipate the heartache that she knew was right around the corner.

The owners of the places she sold her fish to always preferred she wait until after the dinner rush to come by, so it was always late in the evening when she parked outside their kitchens and sold to them.

The first place she went was to the café. She pulled up in front of the back door where light spilled out into the alley and two young men in hairnets stood just outside smoking cigarettes.

Josie got out of the truck and opened her tailgate. "Can one of you guys tell Marie that Josie is out here?"

"Sure." One of them tossed down his cigarette and ground it out with his heel, then disappeared back into the café kitchen.

The fish were displayed in big coolers filled with

just enough water to keep them alive. It wasn't long before Marie Boujoulais came outside. The large woman had a plump face, a sweet smile and a shock of white hair.

"Evening, Josie," she said with a big smile. Despite her smiles, Josie knew the older woman had a will of steel. She ran the restaurant with an iron hand, yet everyone who worked for her adored her.

"Evening, Marie. I think you'll be happy with what I have for you tonight. I've got a beauty of a catfish caught fresh this morning, along with more nice fish."

"Let me get a good look at what you have." Marie moved closer to the back of the truck.

Marie had always been very kind to Josie, but she loved to dicker and drove a hard bargain. Still, Josie was a savvy business woman and wasn't about to allow Marie to get one over on her.

It took about fifteen minutes for the two to finally agree on what fish Marie wanted to buy and for how much. The fish were unloaded and then from there, Josie drove to Tremont's.

She once again pulled up to the back kitchen door. It was Joseph Tremont, a dapper older man who owned the restaurant, who came out to buy from her. He never argued over Josie's prices and bought what he wanted.

Finally, the last stop was the grocery store. The back door was located at the top of a shipping dock. Complete darkness had now fallen as she climbed the stairs to go into the back door, which led into a large storeroom.

To the left was the butcher area. It was enclosed in glass and there was a bell for her to ring to get the attention of Ed Moren, the head butcher.

He immediately came out and greeted her with a wide smile. “It’s good to see you, Josie. How are you doing?”

“I can’t complain,” she replied.

“I’m about out of all my fish supply so I hope you’ve got plenty for me.”

“I’ve got an ice chest full for you out in my truck,” she replied.

“Let me grab a couple of my men and one of our chests and we’ll meet you out there,” he said.

Minutes later, the fish had been removed from her cooler and she’d been paid. She hurried down the steps to get back to her truck. She was ready to get home before it rained and the scent of rain was definitely in the air.

She had just reached the driver’s door when she felt a looming presence behind her. Before she could turn to see who was there, a hard punch slammed into the center of her back. Her breath whooshed out of her and she grabbed the truck door handle to keep from falling to the ground.

Another fist banged into the side of her head, making her brain reel with dizziness as pain seared through her. Wha-what was happening? Who was hitting her? And why? Before he could hit her again, she managed to whirl around. It was a man in a black ski mask, the same man who had chased her through the swamp. Oh, God, what did he want from her? Why was he doing this to her?

Her brain couldn't work properly as terror clutched her. He punched her in her belly and once again all the air left her lungs and she went down to the hot asphalt.

She scooted back from him and at the same time she fumbled to get her knife out. She managed to pull it out and held it out before her. He didn't even hesitate, but kicked her hand and the knife went skittering and spinning away from her.

He booted her in the head once again. A sky full of stars shot off in her vision, momentarily blinding her. He kicked her again in the stomach. Pain seared through her and she felt like she was going to throw up.

God, if she didn't do something quickly, he was going to beat her to death. How did she protect herself against a raging bull? She cast a quick glance around, seeking some kind of help. But the parking lot was empty. There was nobody around to help her.

She finally found her voice and screamed, but the sound was thin and faint amid the sobs of pain that also released from her. She screamed again and this time it was a little bit louder.

He began to pummel her, fists to the side of her face and head in a fury. She screamed over and over again, fearful that he was killing her. Tears of pain blinded her as she moved around on the ground in an effort to get away from him.

She smelled his rage as he continued to hit and kick her. Finally, she curled up in a fetal position in an attempt to survive, but that didn't stop him from the attack.

"Die, you bitch," he growled. "You need to die right now, you swamp scum," he said as he kicked her yet again.

She screamed once more, but it sounded to her ears like a mere whimper.

"Hey…what's going on out there," an unfamiliar voice yelled from the loading dock.

Just as quickly the attack stopped and the sound of running footsteps was the last thing she heard as darkness completely claimed her.

HE RAN AS fast and as furiously as he could away from the parking lot. His heart pounded hard in his chest and his breathing released from him in short deep gasps.

Dammit. He was so ticked off that some damn stocker boy had halted his beatdown on the swamp slut. If he'd had just a few more minutes with her, he would have been able to kill her or at the very least turn her into a vegetable that had to be fed and babbled nothing but nonsense. He could only hope he'd done enough damage to her that she would just die from all her injuries.

It had been a gift from God that he'd been on his

way to the grocery store and saw her truck going into the back parking lot.

He'd parked in the front lot and then ran around the store and hid in the deep shadows behind one of the trash dumpsters in the back. He'd watched as she conducted her business with the butcher and then when she'd come back out to leave, he'd pounced on her.

With his first punch, an enormous rage toward her had taken over him. How dare she come out of the swamp and hook up with his best friend. How dare she play in his playground when she should be deep in the swamp where she belonged.

He finally stopped running and leaned against a tree trunk in somebody's dark front yard. He bent over with his hands on his knees to catch his breath and then checked his knuckles to see what kind of damage he had done to himself.

Thankfully, he had big meaty hands and he didn't think they looked too bad despite the numerous times he had hit her. Besides, he had kicked her more than he had punched her.

God, it had felt so good to unload on her. Beating her felt almost as good as that night when he'd encountered her in the swamp.

He began the long trek back through a neighborhood so he could get to the front door of the supermarket. He still had to buy some groceries before heading home.

He hoped it had been enough. He hoped like hell

that he'd beaten her hard enough that she would die. He wanted so much for her to be dead. She could destroy his life. But he absolutely couldn't allow that to happen.

If his beatdown of her tonight hadn't killed her, then he'd come up with another plan to assure her death. He entered the grocery store and grabbed a cart. He smiled at one of the checkout girls and then went up the first aisle.

Oh, yeah, one way or another, the swamp slut would never get an opportunity to identify him as her attacker.

JACKSON HAD JUST gotten into bed when his cell phone rang. The caller identification was an unfamiliar number, but he decided to answer it anyway.

"Is this Jackson Fortier?" a feminine voice asked.

"It is," he replied.

"This is Amy Stein, I'm a nurse here at the hospital and we have a patient here who is requesting your presence."

Jackson frowned, wondering if this was some kind of a mix-up. "Uh...who is the patient?"

"Josephine Cadieux."

He shot up in the bed. Josie? "Why is she at the hospital?" A million things raced through his head, none of them good. "What is her condition?"

"I'm sorry, I can't discuss that with you. I was just given instructions and told to let you know that she's asking for you."

"Okay, thank you." Jackson hung up and flew into action. He dressed quickly, grabbed his keys and ran out of his house. As he drove toward the hospital, his nerves were taut and he felt sick to his stomach. What could have possibly happened to her? Why in God's name was she in the hospital and what was her condition?

Had she fallen and broken a bone? Had the Honey Island Swamp Monster attempted to make her his fourth victim and somehow she'd managed to escape from him but was wounded? Jeez, how wounded was she?

At least she'd been able to give them his name, but that hardly made him feel better. Was it an accident that had put her in the hospital or something far more nefarious?

He wheeled into the hospital parking lot, halted his engine and then bolted from the car. He flew into the emergency waiting room and immediately approached the desk. A woman he didn't know was seated behind a glass window. She opened the window and smiled at him. "May I help you?"

"Josephine Cadieux was brought in earlier. A nurse called me and said she was asking for me."

"Ah, yes, you must be Jackson," she replied. "She's in bay three. You can go on back." She punched a button and double doors allowed him to enter into the proper emergency room. There were only four bays inside with curtains hung as a measure of privacy.

The first two bays he passed were empty. He entered the third and stopped in his tracks. She was in the bed and her eyes were closed. An IV was in her wrist and she looked small and frail. He'd never seen her so utterly still and it broke his heart.

He quietly walked over to a chair at the side of the bed and sank down. What was going on? What had happened to her? She turned her head toward him and he saw a darkening on the side of her face. What the hell? It looked like she'd been hit and hit hard.

Her eyes fluttered open. She stared at him for a long moment and then began to cry. "Oh, baby, don't cry." He jumped to his feet and hovered over her, wanting to pull her into his arms but afraid to until he found out what had happened to her and how badly she was hurt.

Instead, he sat back down and scooted his chair closer, then took her hand in his. "Josie…honey, please don't cry."

"Oh, J-Jackson. It…it was so terr-terrible," she said amid her tears.

"What, honey? What was terrible? Tell me what happened to you?" he asked.

At that moment, Dr. Etienne Richards walked into the bay. The doctor greeted Jackson with a friendly nod. The two men had occasionally double-dated in the past and hung out on other social occasions. Josie finally managed to get her tears under control.

"Just as I suspected, Josie, along with the concussion, you have three cracked ribs, but thankfully there doesn't seem to be any other internal damage," he said.

A concussion? Three cracked ribs? "Can somebody please tell me what happened?" Jackson asked.

"Apparently, somebody tried to beat the hell out of Josie at the grocery store this evening," Etienne said.

"What?" Jackson looked from Etienne to Josie.

"He was trying to kill me, Jackson." Tears filled her eyes once again. "I… I swear he wanted to kill me. He…he told me to die wh-while he was beating me."

"Who, honey? Did you see who did this to you?"

"A man in a black ski mask," she replied. Her lips trembled and her eyes darkened.

"Like the man who chased you through the swamp," Jackson replied. His blood boiled at the thought of Josie being hit by anyone. It was now apparent to him that somebody was targeting her specifically. Why?

He had a lot of questions about what had happened tonight, but now wasn't the time to ask them. She was obviously in a lot of pain and now it was time for the doctor to speak.

"I'm going to keep you overnight," he said. "We'll monitor you to make sure there aren't any more issues. Unfortunately, there's nothing I can do about your cracked ribs. They'll just have to heal up on their own. I will give you some pain medicine, but because of your concussion, it will have to be a fairly light dose."

Etienne looked at Jackson. "You can see her tomorrow. I'm going to get her moved to a hospital room and right now, what she needs more than anything is rest and that means no visitors until tomorrow."

Jackson nodded his understanding. While he didn't want to leave her side, he wanted to do what was best for her. He stood and leaned over and gently kissed her forehead. "Josie, I'll see you tomorrow."

"Okay." She released a shuddering deep sigh and closed her eyes.

Jackson motioned for Etienne to step out of the bay with him. He waited to say anything until they were far enough away that Josie wouldn't hear them.

"Were the police called about this?" he asked the doctor.

Etienne nodded. "Officer Ryan Staub was here right before you arrived. He questioned her for a few minutes and then left to go check out the parking lot where she was attacked." He shook his head. "I've got to tell you, Jackson. Somebody really did a number on her and if the attack hadn't been interrupted, I don't even want to think about all the life-threatening injuries she could have suffered."

Jackson's heart squeezed tight as he thought about Josie's pain. He hoped like hell the police caught the person responsible. "What I'm worried about right now is her safety going forward. I know there's no real security here at the hospital, so I'd like to sit outside of her hospital room door for the night. Would you have a problem with that?"

Etienne frowned. "I guess that wouldn't be a problem, as long as you stay out of her room and let her rest until morning. Jackson, she's been through a tremendous trauma and her mind and body needs a time-out."

"Can you tell me what hospital room you're putting her in?"

"It's going to be room five. It will take us about twenty minutes to get her transferred there."

"Then I'm going to run home real quick and I'll be right back," Jackson replied.

He didn't wait for any more conversation but rather he turned on his heels and hurried out of the emergency room. He drove back home as fast as he could. The first thing he did was make himself a cup of coffee, which he poured into a to-go cup. The second thing he did was grab his gun from his nightstand.

He slid on his holster and put the gun where it belonged and then pulled on a sports jacket to hide the fact that he wore the gun.

He carried his coffee to his car and then headed back to the hospital. As he drove, a million questions roared through his head.

Why had some man targeted Josie? The same person had gone after her twice now. Why would anyone want her dead? Who had stopped the attack? And had they seen something that might lead to the identity of the person who had beaten her?

Gravois and his men better be fully engaged in

investigating this. Jackson tightened his hands on the steering wheel. If he caught the creep before he was arrested, he would beat the hell out of the man for hurting Josie. Jackson would make sure the man felt as much pain as Josie had.

His heart squeezed tight as he thought of her condition. He couldn't imagine the pain she must have gone through…must still be going through. How many times had she been hit? How many times had she been kicked? He couldn't imagine a man doing that to any woman. But why Josie?

The thing that bothered him the most was if that man meant to beat her to death, then he hadn't succeeded. That meant he was probably going to try to kill her again.

Not if Jackson could help it. He had a gun and a plan that would assure that nobody got close to Josie a second time.

When he got back to the hospital, he double-checked that his sports coat hid his gun. On the front of the building was a sign that no guns were allowed inside, but there wasn't adequate security here. The creep could just waltz in and find her and try to finish the job he had started.

He walked in through the main entrance and found room five where a folding chair was sitting just outside it.

Before he sat, he peeked inside. She was in the bed and appeared to be asleep. Assured that she was okay, he sank down in the chair and took a sip from his coffee cup.

Again, a thousand questions rolled around in his head, the main recurring one was who was responsible for this? If it was the same man who had chased her through the swamp, then he had to have somehow followed her to find her at the supermarket. Who…and why?

He leaned his head back and released a deep sigh. He was still shocked and angered by the events of the night. It was too late tonight to make any phone calls, but first thing in the morning he intended to phone Gravois to see exactly what was being done.

He also had to remember to call his buddies to cancel tomorrow night. There was no way Josie would be in any shape tomorrow for a social gathering.

In fact, it was going to take her some time to heal. God, he wished he would have been there with her. Then none of this would have ever happened. Thank God her attacker hadn't had a gun or a knife. This thought shot an icy chill up his spine.

He must have fallen asleep for he jerked awake at the sound of somebody coming down the hallway. He relaxed when he saw it was a nurse. She smiled at him and then went into Josie's room. As she went in, Jackson got out of his chair and he stood at the doorway and watched her as she checked Josie's vitals. Once she was finished and had left the room, he relaxed again in the chair.

When he finally opened his eyes for good, it was

to daylight creeping through the nearby windows and the sounds of the hospital waking up. He stood and stretched and peeked into the room where Josie still appeared to be sleeping.

He felt surprisingly refreshed, considering that his light sleep had been interrupted several times by hospital staff coming or going down the hallway. He'd have liked a cup of coffee, but he wasn't about to leave his post. Anybody could walk into the hospital and find her. He didn't want to leave her unguarded for a minute.

It was only when a pleasant older woman wheeled in a cart that smelled of breakfast that he followed her into the room. "Here you go, sweetheart," the woman said as she set a tray of food on the table that swung over the bed. "You've got some scrambled eggs and bacon and an orange juice and coffee."

"Thank you," Josie replied. She raised the head of her bed and grimaced slightly.

"I'll be back later for your tray," the woman said and then she left the room.

Jackson sat in the chair next to the bed and eyed her worriedly. The side of her face was definitely bruised and he imagined she was also badly bruised beneath the blue-flowered hospital gown. "Josie… baby, how are you doing this morning?"

"Okay, except I feel like several big trucks ran over me."

"Honey, I'm so sorry this happened to you."

Her eyes flashed darkly. "He was filled with such

rage, Jackson. He came at me out of nowhere and beat and kicked me. My knife was no defense at all. The minute I pulled it, he kicked it out of my hand. He kicked and hit me in such a flurry that I couldn't do anything to protect myself."

"Baby, don't think about it right now," he said. "Thank God you survived."

"If it weren't for a stocker who saw what was happening and yelled, I truly don't believe I would have survived. He would have killed me. He would have beat me to death."

"Thank God for that stocker, now eat your breakfast before it gets cold," he said.

She frowned. "I'm really not very hungry."

"Josie, you need to eat to keep up your strength. You have a lot of healing to do."

She picked up her fork and took a bite of her eggs, then took a drink of her orange juice. "You want my coffee? I'm not in the mood for it."

"If you're sure you don't want it, then I'll drink it."

"Go for it," she replied.

He had just taken his first drink of the hot brew when Etienne walked in. "Good morning," he said in greeting and immediately looked at Jackson. "How are you faring after last night?" he asked.

"I'm a little stiff, but I'm all right," Jackson replied.

"Wait…what did you do last night?" Josie asked in obvious confusion.

"He sat outside your door in a folding chair all night," Etienne said. "Now that's what I call devotion."

"Oh, Jackson," she said and tears filled her eyes.

"Hey, it was no big deal. I was just worried about you," he said quickly, not wanting to see her cry. "Please, don't worry about it."

"And how's my patient today?" Etienne asked Josie.

"I've definitely been better," she said. "But I'm ready to go home."

"Whoa, I'm not quite ready to release you yet," Etienne protested. "How about we keep you a little while longer and see how you're doing after lunch today."

"Okay," Josie replied.

"Then let's just do a quick checkup right now." Etienne listened to her heart, used a flashlight to look into her eyes and then left the room.

"As soon as he releases you, I'll take you home, but you aren't going to stay there," Jackson said. "We'll pack up a couple of bags for you and then you're coming to my place to stay while you heal."

"Jackson… I…"

"Please don't argue with me, Josie." He took her hand and squeezed it tight. "Somebody definitely tried to kill you last night and he didn't succeed, which means he'll come after you again. You need a bodyguard and I want that position. I'll make sure nobody hurts you again."

She stared into his eyes and tears filled hers. Was she going to reject his offer? He knew she was not only a strong woman, but a prideful one as well. "Josie, please," he said softly. "If nothing else, do this for me."

"Just for a couple of days while I get my strength back," she finally agreed.

"Good, then it's settled." He squeezed her hand one more time and then released it.

She'd agreed to a couple of days, but he intended to keep her with him until the police caught the creep that was after her. And after that, he was hoping to keep her with him forever.

Chapter Eight

It wasn't just the physical pain that had Josie uncomfortable, but it was emotional pain as well. She knew who had attacked her the night before. It was the same man who had raped her months before. She knew that because he had smelled exactly the same and she'd recognized his voice… The voice that had haunted her dreams for what felt like forever.

Once she got settled in at Jackson's, she intended to tell him that. More, she knew it was time she come clean with him about why she'd started her relationship with him in the first place. She knew it was going to hurt him, but he deserved to know the truth before he offered her any more help.

She couldn't believe that he'd sat outside her room all night long. He was obviously worried about her safety. His vigilance through the night touched her heart more deeply than anything had in her entire life.

She now turned on the television to pass the time until the doctor would return and hopefully release her. However, the TV didn't stop them from talking and they had only been talking a few minutes when she saw the gun at Jackson's waist.

"You have a gun?" she asked in surprise although it was a rhetorical question. "Why do you have it here?"

"I was worried about the person who attacked you last night creeping into the hospital to finish the job, so I ran home and got my gun and then came back to sit outside your doorway." His eyes narrowed slightly. "Nobody was going to get into your room last night except hospital staff."

"Jackson, I'll never be able to thank you enough," she said, her heart once again touched by his words and actions.

He cast her one of his gentle smiles. "You don't have to thank me, honey. I don't want you to ever get hurt like this again and I'm here to make sure that nothing else ever happens to you."

They chatted a little bit longer and then she must have fallen asleep.

She was back in time…back to that horrible night. A dark bag fell over her head, half-choking her. Fear shot through her as she was shoved from behind. She was flipped over as if she weighed nothing at all and then soft male hands grabbed hers with the intent to tie her up. No…no! This couldn't be happening.

"Honey… Josie…wake up." The male voice sliced through the nightmare. The soft sweetly familiar voice she knew. She opened her eyes to see Jackson standing over her, a worried expression on his handsome face.

"Oh, I'm sorry… Did…did I scream out?" she asked with embarrassment.

"No, not at all. But it looked and sounded like you weren't enjoying your nap."

"I wasn't. I was having a nightmare." She moved her bed so that she was sitting up once again. "Thank you for waking me. How long was I asleep?"

He sat back down in the chair. "About an hour and a half."

"Really?" She shook her head. "I almost never nap."

"You'll probably be napping a lot in the next couple of days. That's the way your body is going to heal itself." He held her gaze for a long moment. "Josie, I only wish I knew who attacked you, because I'd beat the holy hell out of him for what he did to you."

"Thank you, Jackson. I appreciate the sentiment." She broke the eye contact with him. If she looked into the depths of his eyes for too long, she would cry again. He loved her. She saw it in his beautiful eyes and felt it in his every touch.

He loved her and she thought if she looked deep in her heart, she would realize she was in love with him, too. But she didn't want to love him.

He was from the town and that scared her. She didn't believe a long-term relationship between them would ever work out. She probably didn't have to worry about it anyway because once she told him the truth about why she'd started pursuing him, he'd probably hate her. She'd be surprised if he took her back to his place to heal and she wanted to be at his house more than anything, at least for a little while.

For the first time in her life, she needed somebody. The attack last night had shaken her to her very core and she was more afraid than she'd ever been. And despite everything else that was whirling around in her head, she wanted…she needed Jackson.

"Do you want to talk about your nightmare?" he now asked.

"I don't have them very often and it's always the same thing. I relive the night of the assault against me, but I don't want to talk about that anymore."

"How about we talk about favorite animals. I've always been partial to the aardvark."

She laughed, and then immediately groaned and wrapped her arms around her middle. "Oh, please don't make me laugh. It makes my ribs hurt."

"Sorry," he replied. "The last thing I want to do is make you hurt more than you already do."

They wound up just small-talking until lunch arrived. "Jackson, help me eat this," she said. "You must be starving."

"I'm okay. I'll eat later when we get you settled in at my place."

If he decided to follow through on the plans after she confessed to him.

It wasn't long after lunch when the doctor came back in. He released her with the condition that she stay in bed and rest for the next week to ten days and after that do only what her body allowed her to do.

Jackson stepped out of the room as a nurse came in to help her dress. A shiver of revulsion shot through her as she pulled on the short-sleeved blouse that was now ripped and dirty. Her jeans had fared better, but were filthy from the scuffle on the parking lot asphalt.

She left the room armed with a handful of paperwork, a prescription for pain meds and a deep dread of what was to come with Jackson.

He cast her a big smile as she walked out of the room. "Okay, toots, let's blow this joint," he said and took her hand in his. "While you were dressing, I pulled my car up front so you won't have to walk too far."

"Thank you," she replied. She was definitely grateful, for every step she took shot pain throughout her body. In fact, just drawing too deep a breath caused her ribs to scream in protest. When she'd dressed, she noticed all kinds of bruises all over her.

She eased down into the passenger seat of his car and released a deep tired sigh. The first thing they did was drive through the pharmacy to get her pain meds and then he headed to Vincent's parking lot so they could go to her place to pack a few things.

Aside from her physical pain, with each mile that passed, her nerves jangled louder and louder inside her. Jackson had always been so very kind to her, among other things, and she knew what she was going to tell him would hurt him and probably hurt him deep. But it was now necessary to come clean to him. Her conscience couldn't hold it in any longer.

When they reached Vincent's, he parked the car and then hurried around to her side to help her out. "I wish I could carry you in, Josie. I wish you didn't even have to go to your place."

"But I do," she replied. She forced a reassuring smile to her lips. "I'll be fine, Jackson. We're just going to have to walk very slowly."

"That's no problem for me," he replied.

Together they entered the tangled growth and forged ahead. She went slowly, each step shooting pain through her. She fought back tears as she realized just how weak and injured she felt.

By the time they reached her shanty, she collapsed on the sofa in exhaustion and pain. Jackson sank down beside her. "Baby, is there anything I can do for you?" he asked, his blue eyes filled with concern.

"No, thanks. I just need a couple of minutes to rest before we head back out," she replied. *If* she left with him, she reminded herself.

"Take all the time you need," he said. "What you do need to do as soon as possible is take one of those pain pills and crawl into a nice soft bed."

"That sounds like heaven right now. But before I can do that, we need to have a talk," she said. Dread built up inside her and pressed tight against her chest.

"Okay...a talk about what?" He looked at her curiously.

"I know the person who attacked me last night. It was the same man who raped me." She looked away from him. "I told you he was somebody from the swamp, but he's not. He's a person from town."

"How do you know that?" he asked, obviously surprised.

She looked back at him. "I know because he has soft hands. Nobody who lives and works in the swamp has hands like that. And I also know because of the way he smells. He smells of expensive cologne. It's a scent of balsam and patchouli. I'll never ever forget it. And both times I heard his voice."

He gazed at her in open confusion. "Then why did you tell me it was somebody from the swamp?"

She released a deep sigh, hating what she was going to tell him next. "Jackson, you know that as somebody from the swamp, I was never going to be in a place to identify him if he was from town. I wasn't welcome in the places where he would be."

Once again, she looked away from him, her heart beating a million miles a minute. "You were like a gift from God, dropped right into the swamp for me."

She gazed back at him. "I started dating you because you were absolutely perfect. I hoped you would take me to those places where I could find my assailant."

The shine in his eyes dimmed. "So basically, you've been using me all along." The hurt in his eyes twisted her heart. Why had she even decided he needed to know this? She should have just broken up with him and never let him know the truth.

"Oh, Jackson, I won't lie. I started out with the intention to use you, but then I grew to care for you and I wanted to spend time with you no matter what we did together. It…you became more than just catching my assailant."

It was true, he had dug himself deep into her heart but eventually she knew she had to let him go. "I'm sorry, Jackson, but I was using you." She reached out and placed her hand on his arm as tears filled her eyes. "I'm so very sorry." A deep sob escaped her.

"Don't cry, Josie. It will only make you hurt more," he replied on a deep sigh. "I just want to know why you decided to tell me all of this right now?"

She swallowed hard against her tears. "I didn't want the lie to be between us anymore. I care about you deeply and I thought you had the right to know."

"So, now you've told me and I think you should go pack a bag before you get more tired and in pain."

"Are you sure you still want me to go with you?"

"Josie, I care about you very much and of course I still want you to go with me. We'll get you healed up and then I'll help you find the man who assaulted you. Now go, get a bag or whatever you need to be away for a while."

She got up from the sofa and then hurried to her bedroom. Once there, she sank down on the side of her bed and began to cry again.

This time the tears were because of Jackson's

never-ending kindness to her, his willingness to take her in despite the fact that she had just told him she had been using him.

Her emotional pain right now was almost as bad as her physical pain, but she pulled herself together and went to her closet. She grabbed a large duffel bag and began to pack what she thought she'd need for a couple days away.

It didn't take long for her to finish. She then went into the bathroom and added her toiletries to the bag. Once that was done, she carried it out into the living room.

Jackson immediately jumped up from the sofa and took the bag from her. "All ready?"

"More ready than you know." She should feel guilty again for going to his place to heal. But she'd never felt so physically and emotionally broken. She also felt more vulnerable than she ever had in her life.

The man who had raped her months ago had tried to kill her last night. There was no doubt he'd wanted her dead. Somehow, she had threatened him. He had to have seen her around town with Jackson and knew she'd entered his world. He wanted to make sure he remained hidden and she jeopardized that.

Together, they left her place. He was unusually quiet and she wondered just how badly she had hurt him. She couldn't think about it now. Maybe it was good she had told him. Maybe this would redefine their relationship so that when the end finally did come, neither of them would be hurt.

By the time they reached his car to go home, Jackson was still trying to process what she had confessed to him. Had it all been a lie?

Had her laughter with him been forced? Had the deep conversations they'd shared only been a bore to her all along? Had the passionate kisses they had shared only been an act on her part?

The fact that Josie needed him now didn't escape him. She was hurt and needed him to help care for her. He'd be there for her because despite what she'd told him, he still loved her and he knew the next few days would be rough ones for her.

He glanced over to her now. She had her head back and her eyes closed. The vivid bruise on the side of her face made his heart squeeze tight and a deep anger rose up inside him. He still couldn't believe somebody had attacked her with such force.

According to her, it had been the same man who had raped her…a man from town. She obviously hadn't run into him on the night of the gala, otherwise she would have identified him.

Maybe what Jackson needed to do now was sit and write a list of everyone she'd encountered at the party and write down all the men who hadn't been there. It would be a daunting task, but he was determined to help her find the person who haunted her dreams and gave her nightmares. He was determined to help find the man who had tried to kill her.

He pulled in and parked at his place. "Josie, we're here."

She straightened up and released a weary sigh. Together, they got out of the car. He grabbed her bag from the back seat and then they headed toward the front door.

"I want you to go in and get relaxed," he said as he unlocked the door.

"Before I do anything, I'd like a shower. I feel dirty. I still feel like his hands are all over me," she replied.

"I'm so sorry, Josie. We can definitely arrange a shower," he replied. He led her toward his guest room and set her bag on the foot of the bed. "Why don't you give me your pain pills and I'll bring you one with a glass of water."

"That sounds wonderful," she replied. Her face was unnaturally pale, her features taut and it was obvious she was in a lot of pain.

She gave him the pill bottle and he took it into the kitchen where he shook one of them out, got a glass of water and then carried them both back to her.

She took the pill and then handed him back the glass. "Thank you." Her gaze held his. "Jackson, thank you for all of this." Tears filled her eyes.

He placed a gentle hand on her shoulder. "Go take your shower and we'll get you settled in. You can use the shower in the bathroom across the hall. Towels are in the linen closet and there is soap there and shampoo under the sink."

"I can't wait to get out of these clothes," she said. "And to feel clean again," she added as she headed to the bathroom. Once she disappeared, he went back into his bedroom and grabbed an extra pillow, a navy throw blanket and a clean sheet.

He carried them all into the living room where he made up a bed on the sofa in case she wanted to rest here instead of in the bedroom. Surely, she wouldn't want to spend all day and all night alone in the bedroom.

He then sank down in the chair opposite the sofa and tried to turn off his whirling thoughts. But it was impossible. Had she always only seen him as a stooge to use? There was no question that his heart hurt a lot, but that hadn't stopped him from wanting to care for her while she was so hurt.

Still, he found himself second-guessing each and every moment the two of them had spent together. Was it possible she'd never really cared for him at all? Was she still just using him?

It didn't take her long in the shower and then she came out wearing black leggings and an oversize blue T-shirt. She still looked pale and weary with pain.

He stood. "Josie, I thought since it's still so early you might want to rest out here, but if you're ready to get into bed, I'll help you turn down the covers."

"No, I'd really like to sit out here with you."

"I don't want you sitting. You need to lie down and as you can see I've got the sofa waiting for you," he replied.

She nodded and stretched out. When she was prone, he covered her up with the blanket and she released a deep sigh. "I'll never be able to thank you enough, Jackson."

He returned to his chair. "Josie, you don't have to keep thanking me. I'm doing this because I want to and because I think you need somebody right now."

"I hate that I'm so weak. I've always been a strong woman who didn't need anyone," she said angrily. "I hate who I am right now."

"I'm assuming you've never been beaten up before," he replied.

"Never. No man has ever laid a hand on me until this man. I think he must have seen me with you and it worried him. That's why he attacked me last night."

"That means he thinks you're getting closer to identifying him, although it pisses me off that being seen with me got you beat up. That also means somebody I know is a rapist." He frowned at that thought. Who could it be?

She didn't say anything in reply. "Why don't we stop talking about all this and I'll put on a movie or something that will let you rest your mind a bit. Or maybe you just prefer the silence," he said.

"A movie would be nice," she replied. "I don't get a chance to watch television or see any movies at home."

He found a movie that he had seen before and that he thought she might enjoy. He turned it on and then settled back in his chair.

Within fifteen minutes, she had fallen asleep. He quietly got up and went into the kitchen. It was going to be dinnertime soon and he decided rather than cooking a big meal, he would fix her a bowl of chicken soup. If she wanted something else, he would figure it out when she woke up. He could always order something and have it delivered.

He then went back into his bedroom, where his voice wouldn't wake her, to call his friends and tell them that tomorrow's gathering wasn't going to happen. They were all shocked at what had happened to Josie and each of them sent her their best.

He returned to the chair in the living room, his thoughts still on his group of friends. Was it possible one of those men was Josie's assailant?

He simply couldn't believe it. There was no way. He knew those men. Brian was happily married and Sonny could probably sleep with any single woman in town. He might have considered Lee because of the man's anger right now, but at the time the attack had occurred Lee had had no idea his marriage was over.

Still, they were three men she hadn't met yet. He'd be glad when she did get to meet them so they could be excluded from the list of potential suspects. The very idea of any one of them being guilty made him feel sick to his stomach.

With that thought in mind, he got up once again and went into the kitchen where a built-in desk held his laptop on the top and in the drawer several notebooks and pens. He grabbed one of the notebooks and pens and then returned to his chair in the living room.

While she was still sleeping, he began to write down the names of all the men who had been at the gala. He believed her attacker had to be of his social status. He was certain the blue-collar workers in town didn't wear expensive cologne or have soft hands.

He'd written down about fifteen names when Josie stirred and came awake. "Hey, sleepyhead," he said.

"I can't believe I fell asleep again," she said.

"I imagine that pain pill had something to do with it," he replied. "Besides, sleep is good for you right now." He set the notebook and his pen on the end table next to his chair. "It's about dinnertime. I was thinking maybe a bowl of chicken noodle soup might sound good to you. My mother always told me it was not only good for the soul but also had magical healing power."

She cast him a faint smile. "Then how can I possibly turn it down?" She sat up and slid her legs off the sofa. "What can I do to help?"

"First of all, we didn't go over the rules of your stay here with me before you went to sleep," he said.

"The rules?" She looked at him in obvious confusion.

"The rules are you stay down and I wait on you hand and foot. Now get back down and I'll have your dinner ready in just a few minutes," he said.

He got up from the chair and hurried to the kitchen where the two cans of the soup awaited him on the countertop. He poured one of the cans in a bowl for her and the second one in a bowl for himself.

As they microwaved, he got out a tray and crackers and spoons. Once the soup was hot, he filled the tray with the bowls and crackers and then carried it back into the living room where he set it on the coffee table.

"What would you like to drink?" he asked. He couldn't help but notice how beautiful she looked despite having just awakened. Her hair was tousled and she wore no makeup, but that only added to her attractiveness. The only thing he hated to see was the dark bruise on the side of her face.

"Nothing to drink for me," she replied. "The soup looks good."

"Yeah, I worked on it all afternoon. The most difficult issue was finding a chicken and when I finally found one, I had to sweet-talk it into my arms without it knowing I was going to stick it in a pot."

A burst of laughter escaped her and she immediately held her sides. "Oh, Jackson, you are good for my soul."

Did she mean that or was she just sweet-talking him because she needed him right now? He shoved the thought out of his head. He couldn't focus on things like that right now, otherwise he'd make himself go crazy.

When they were finished eating, he took the dishes back to the kitchen and put them in the dishwasher and the crackers back into his pantry.

He then returned to the living room. He switched

the television to a show for them to watch and the evening hours went by quickly.

It was about eight thirty when she indicated she was ready to go to bed. He went back into the bedroom with her and turned down the bed as she went across the hall and into the bathroom.

He flipped on the small lamp on the nightstand and she reentered the room clad in a sleeveless light blue nightgown that fell to her knees. As she swept past him, he caught her scent, that ever-present evocative fragrance of floral and fauna and mysterious spices.

"Get into bed and I'll bring you another pill," he said.

She nodded and he turned and hurried back to the kitchen where he got a pain pill and a glass of water.

She took the pill and then settled back in the bed and released a deep sigh. "You can turn off the lamp whenever you're ready," he said and moved back to the doorway. "If you need anything at all through the night, don't hesitate to wake me. Otherwise, I'll just see you in the morning."

"Good night, Jackson."

"Sleep well, Josie."

He left her room and went back into the living room. He watched television for another hour or so and then shut it off, made sure the place was locked up tight and then headed for his own room.

The light in her room was still on but she was once again sleeping. He stood at the threshold of the room and simply gazed at her. His love for her ached deep inside him. He no longer knew what to do with the emotion, because he had no idea what she really felt about him.

He finally walked into his bedroom and sank down on the edge of his bed. Her confession about why she had been interested in him in the first place rang in his ears and through his heart.

She'd said she'd grown to care about him, but how much? And was that even true? He had a feeling he'd better hold on to his heart. It was time he figured out how to stop loving Josie.

Chapter Nine

Josie awakened to the scent of bacon and with pain rocking through her entire body. She remained in bed for several long minutes, grateful that Jackson was apparently fixing breakfast and would have a pain pill for her.

Thankfully, she had slept without dreams, but the sleep hadn't left her feeling well-rested and refreshed. In fact, she hurt more this morning than she had the day before.

She finally pulled herself out of the bed, grabbed a pair of shorts and a T-shirt from her bag along with her toiletry case and then went across the hall to the bathroom.

She changed her clothes, brushed her teeth and hair, and then ready to face the day she headed for the kitchen. Every step she took was still painful. Although most of the beating had been to her head and stomach, her whole body ached.

"Good morning," Jackson greeted her cheerfully when she stepped into the kitchen.

"Good morning to you," she replied and sank down on one of the chairs at the table.

"Coffee?" he asked.

"Please, and a pain pill would be great," she replied.

"Coming right up." He got her the coffee and pill and then returned to the stove and began removing bacon strips from the skillet.

"I certainly don't want to get dependent on this medication," she said after taking one of the pills.

"Give yourself a break, Josie. You only got out of the hospital yesterday and right now you need them," he replied. He looked very handsome this morning in a pair of jeans and a royal blue T-shirt that reminded her he had a very hot physique.

"Now, tell me how you like your eggs," he said as he got the eggs out of the fridge. "How about a nice cheese and mushroom omelet?"

"That sounds wonderful," she replied. "I didn't know you were such a man of many talents. When did you learn to cook?"

"My mom is a great cook and she made sure I knew my way around the kitchen by the time I was a teenager. She told me it was a survival skill that every man should know."

"Your mother is obviously a smart woman," she replied. She sipped her coffee and watched as he prepared the omelet, along with toast.

Once the large omelet was done, he cut it in half, placed each half on separate plates and set them, along with bacon and toast, on the table.

"This is delicious," she said after taking her first couple of bites.

"Good, I'm glad you like it. How did you sleep?" he asked.

"I slept like a baby," she replied. "The bed is very comfortable."

"Good, I'm glad you slept well." His gaze was so warm, so caring as it lingered on her. How could he look at her that way after what she had confessed to him?

She broke the eye contact and focused on eating again. "You know, I've been thinking about the list of potential suspects," he said after a few moments, drawing her attention back to him and away from her plate.

"What about them?" she asked.

"Yesterday while you were napping, I started writing down all the names of the men you met at the gala and then I thought about it after I went to bed last night and realized I probably don't have to worry about the married men in town."

She frowned at him. "And why is that?"

"I would assume that most married men are having intimate relationships with their wives and so wouldn't need to go out and seek sex anywhere else."

She set the piece of toast she was about to bite into back on her plate and released a small laugh. "Oh, Jackson, rape isn't about sex."

He looked at her in obvious confusion. "If it's not about sex, then what's it about?"

"Power," she replied. "It's all about power and

control. That's what a rapist gets off on. It's about overpowering a woman and taking away her choices. The sex really has very little to do with it."

"I never really thought about it that way before, but now that you told me that, I guess it makes sense. So, my list will include both single and married men."

"Sounds like a lot of work," she said.

"I don't consider it work at all. Just call me Sherlock Holmes. I'm determined to find this guy for you, Josie. He needs to be in jail for what he's done to you."

She reached up and touched the side of her face. Her bruise looked worse today than it had yesterday. It was a vivid purple and ached relentlessly.

"You wear the color well," he said.

"Purple has always been one of my favorite colors," she replied dryly. She picked up the piece of toast once again and for the next few minutes they ate the breakfast in silence. When they were finished eating, he insisted she go back to the sofa and relax.

For the next three days, they fell into an easy routine. He fixed her meals and when she wasn't eating in the kitchen with him, she was on the sofa.

They shared long talks and watched movies together. She napped in the afternoons, unable to help herself. However, the naps got shorter when she quit taking her pain pills and started to feel a little better. The one thing they didn't discuss was their feelings for one another.

She thought she sensed a little distance coming from him, but she couldn't be sure. He was still very attentive and determined to take care of her and if he had distanced himself a little from her, she certainly understood why.

The better she felt, the more she wanted him to take her in his arms and tell her he forgave her and to assure her that she was forever safe from the man who hunted her.

She so wanted the warmth of his close embrace, and if she were perfectly honest with herself, she wanted to see the flames of desire back in his eyes as he gazed at her.

She knew her emotions were all over the place where he was concerned. At this point, she was trying not to overthink things. The best thing she could do was finish healing up and get back to the swamp. Surely, in the swamp she would be able to think more clearly about everything.

Meanwhile Jackson had continued making the list of all the men she'd met at the gala and had moved on to making a list of all the men she had yet to meet in town.

It was just a little after seven in the evening of the fourth day that she'd been at his place when Gravois showed up. Jackson led the lawman into the living room where Josie was on the sofa.

Josie knew that Jackson had called the man several times over the past couple of days but each time he'd been told that Gravois was unavailable.

She sat up so he could sit on the other end of the sofa while Jackson sat back in his chair. "Just the man I've been wanting to talk to," Jackson said once they were all settled.

"I'm sorry I haven't contacted you sooner." He looked at Josie. "And, Josie, I hope you are feeling better."

"How is she supposed to feel any better when there's somebody out there who wants to kill her? Somebody who tried to beat her to death just a couple of nights ago?" Jackson asked, his voice deep with a touch of anger. "I hope to hell you brought us some news about the assault."

"Unfortunately, I have no news for you. I spoke to Mac Aris, the stocker who stopped the attack, but the only thing he saw was a man running away from the scene," Gravois said. "He described him as medium height and weight and clad all in black, but could tell us nothing more specific. He was the only witness I could find and without a better description, there isn't much I can do. I'm sorry I don't have better news."

"Did you and your men go over the parking lot where this happened?" Jackson asked.

"We went over every inch of it, hoping that the perpetrator might have dropped something that would lead to his identity, but we found nothing except trash," Gravois replied. "Like I said, I'm sorry I don't have anything for you, but it isn't like we didn't try."

"And I guess you never had anything for Josie when she was raped." Once again, Jackson's voice held a tightly suppressed but discernable anger.

Gravois looked at him in surprise. "That was a long time ago."

"I remember it as if it were yesterday," she said, finding her voice for the first time since Gravois had arrived.

"What exactly did you do when Josie came to you and told you she'd been assaulted that time?" Jackson asked.

"Well, I did the best I could to investigate it," Gravois replied defensively.

"And what exactly did that investigation entail," Jackson pressed as she eyed the man with distaste.

"Well…uh… I would have to go over my notes about that," he replied, obviously flustered by the question. "I just came over now to check in on Josie and update the two of you." He stood, obviously eager now to leave.

Jackson got up as well and walked Gravois to the front door. Josie remained sitting up and exhaled a deep breath of resentment.

Did she believe Gravois had done everything possible to catch the man who had beaten her? The answer was no. Did she believe the man had done anything to investigate her rape? Absolutely not. He hadn't even asked for her clothing to collect DNA.

She heard Jackson's and Gravois's voices coming from the entryway, but they were only a deep mumbling as she was too far away to hear their exact words.

Not that any of it mattered. Gravois wasn't about

to change his lazy ways, not for a mere swamp slut. She'd told him that night when she'd gone to the police station that she was certain her assailant was a man from town and Gravois wasn't about to arrest one of his own.

She heard the front door close and then Jackson came back into the room. "I'd love to see that man leave town and never come back," he said as he sank back down in his chair. "As soon as all of this is over, I'm leading a recall effort to get him out of office for good. He's nothing but a disgrace and it's past time for him to go."

She was surprised that Jackson's anger warmed her inside. She knew it was on her behalf and that he was fighting for justice for her. In fact, over the last couple of days, a desire for him had built up inside her. As her body healed, it yearned for something more… It yearned for him.

His scent was everywhere in the house, on the blanket she used to nap on the sofa, on the sheets she slept on each night. It was a redolent smell of clean masculinity and ocean fresh air. It was a smell that made her feel safe and protected and welled up a desire for him that she couldn't deny.

For the next few minutes, he talked to her about what was needed to get Gravois out of office. "Who would take his place?" she asked curiously.

"We would have to have a special election and it depends on who runs for the position." He frowned. "I think the whole department stinks. Gravois told me before he left that he had placed ads in the Shreveport and New Orleans papers seeking a new hire for the department. Maybe a new guy coming in fresh will make a good chief of police."

"It would be nice if he came in with no prejudices and gave equal justice to the townspeople and to the people who live in the swamps," she replied.

"We're not going to put up with anything else but that," he replied firmly.

She offered him a smile. "You've become quite a justice warrior."

He returned her smile. "Thanks to you. You've opened my eyes to a lot of things, Josie. What was acceptable before is no longer acceptable now. There has to be changes made."

For a long moment, their gazes remained locked and in the depths of his beautiful blue eyes she saw a flickering flame that called to a heat that filled her.

He broke the eye contact and picked up the remote for the television. "Ready to watch something?"

She didn't want to watch television. She wanted Jackson to take her into his arms and kiss her until she was mindless. She wanted him to make love to her. Her body, soul and mind were ready for it to happen tonight.

"Actually, I'm ready for bed," she said and got up from the sofa. Her heart took on an accelerated rhythm. He immediately got up from his chair. Each night when she'd gone to bed, he'd walked her to the bedroom door to tell her good-night.

Together, they went down the hallway and when they reached the door, she turned back to face him. "Good night, Josie," he said. "I hope you sleep well."

She took a step closer to him, her heart now thundering in her chest. Since she'd told him that initially she'd been using him, maybe he wouldn't want her anymore. But she definitely wanted him right now.

"Jackson, I told you I was ready for bed, but the last thing on my mind is sleep." She took another step toward him, now standing so close to him their bodies almost touched.

"Josie." Her name fell from his lips on a whispered sigh as the fire in his eyes ignited.

"I want you, Jackson," she said boldly.

"Josie, you're hurt," he replied faintly.

"I'm better now, Jackson, and I want to make love with you." She reached her arms up and placed them on his shoulders. With a small groan, he gently pulled her into his embrace. "Kiss me, Jackson," she whispered softly. "Please kiss me."

He touched his lips to hers in a tender kiss that not only stirred her desire for him, but also touched her very heart. She deepened the kiss, dipping her tongue in to swirl with his.

The kiss went on for several long moments, and then she broke the embrace, grabbed his hand and led him into the bedroom. The lamp next to the bed was on, creating a small golden pool of illumination that couldn't begin to compete with the flames that burned in his eyes…the flames that burned deep inside her.

Once they were by the bed, she stepped back from him and pulled the T-shirt she wore over her head. She tossed it to the floor next to them and then moved back into his arms.

This time when he kissed her, she tasted his wild hunger for her and that only stoked the flames of want higher inside her. His warm hands caressed the bare skin of her back, shooting shivers of delight through her.

Despite her excitement, she felt safe…so wonderfully safe in his arms. There were no alarm bells ringing in her head, no hint of a flashback or anything to stop her from the physical act of making love with Jackson.

They finally broke apart and she reached behind her and unfastened her bra. It fell to the floor in front of her. "Oh, Josie, you are so beautiful," he said softly.

"I want to feel your naked chest next to mine," she said. Once again, she stepped close to him and began to unbutton his shirt. She held his gaze as her hands undressed him. The intense eye contact felt almost as intimate as the actual act of lovemaking.

Once his shirt was unbuttoned, she shoved it off his broad shoulders and it fell to the floor behind him. His chest was magnificent, firmly muscled and solid.

He stood before her yet made no move to touch her in any way. It was then she realized he was allowing her to take the lead. The fact that he was thinking about her despite his own physical desire once again touched her heart deeply.

She slid her shorts down her legs and then, clad only in her panties, she got into the bed. He hesitated only a moment and then took off the slacks he'd been wearing, leaving him wearing only a pair of black boxers. He joined her beneath the sheets and their bodies came together as he took her lips with his in a searing kiss.

His bare skin felt wonderful against her own and as his hands cupped her breasts, she wanted more… so much more. She rolled over on her back as his lips left her mouth and slid down her neck in nipping kisses.

Finally, his mouth reached one of her nipples. He licked and sucked, creating a coil of electricity that raced from her breasts to the very center of her.

She was quickly lost in him…in them. As he continued to give attention to her nipples, she ran her hands from his rich soft hair down his back, loving the play of his hard muscles beneath his soft skin.

He moved one hand down to her stomach and then stopped, as if hesitant to go any farther. "Touch me, Jackson," she whispered breathlessly. "It's okay. I want you to touch me everywhere."

He released a groan at her words and his hand slid farther down her stomach. He reached the top of her panties and ran his hand from one side to the other and back again, teasing and tormenting her. He finally touched her where she most wanted, moving his fingers to dance over the silk of her panties.

She gasped as sheer pleasure rocked through her, but it still wasn't enough for her. She pushed against him and he immediately stopped what he was doing. She shoved her panties down and kicked them off, then pulled him back toward her.

This time when he touched her, wild sensations sparked through her and shot a growing tension that had her panting for release. Higher and higher she climbed, and when that release finally came, she cried out his name in deep gasps.

Still, even then, she wanted more from him. She plucked at his boxers, wanting them off him. He complied and took them off and she pushed him on his back. He was fully aroused and she encircled him with her hand, loving the pulsating hardness of him.

"Josie, you're driving me wild," he said with a deep groan.

In answer, she crawled on top of him and once in position, she then lowered herself onto him. He groaned again and she moaned with pleasure. For several long moments she didn't move, simply reveling in the way he filled her up so completely.

When she did finally move, his hands held onto her hips as she rose up and down on his hard length. Once again, their gazes locked as they shared the utter intimacy of the moment.

She pumped up and down, faster and faster as a new tension inside her rose higher and higher. Her climax slammed into her at the same time he cried out her name and found his own release.

She collapsed on her back next to him, unable to speak as she waited for her breathing to return to normal. He was also catching his breath and neither of them spoke for several long moments.

He then rolled to his side facing her. "Are you okay?" he asked with a touch of concern in his voice.

She smiled at him. "I'm more than okay."

He reached out and gently shoved a strand of her hair away from her cheek. "You're an amazing woman, Josie."

"This amazing woman will be right back," she replied and rolled out of the bed. She grabbed her nightgown and hurried into the bathroom across the hall.

She hadn't thought she would ever make love again. She'd believed that part of her had been stolen away from her, taken in a single night of violence.

She knew without a doubt that Jackson was the reason she'd found her desire again. It had been his kindness, his tenderness and the wealth of love that shone from his eyes that had made her feel safe enough to go there again.

Pulling her nightgown over her head, the press of tears burned at her eyes. She swallowed hard against them and then left the bathroom.

Jackson wasn't in the bedroom. His boxers were missing from the floor so she assumed he'd gone back to the bathroom in his bedroom.

She got back into the bed and a moment later he appeared in the doorway. She hadn't wanted to bask in the afterglow of their lovemaking and she didn't want to spend the rest of the night with him holding her.

She didn't want his arms around her or his breathing to mingle with hers as she drifted off to sleep. It would be far too painful for her to have those memories.

He remained at the threshold, obviously waiting for her to invite him back in. "Jackson, if you don't mind, I'd like to sleep alone."

"Of course," he replied instantly. "Josie…did I hurt you?"

"Not at all, but I'm still a bit achy and just prefer to be alone to finish out the night."

"Then I'll just say good-night and I'll see you in the morning," he replied.

"Good night, Jackson." The minute he was gone from the doorway, she reached out and turned off the lamp. The room was dark except for the faint moonlight that shone through the window.

The tears that had burned at her eyes in the bathroom now seeped out once again. She wished she could have let him come back into the bedroom to sleep with her, but as crazy as it sounded after what they had just shared, she hadn't wanted the memory of falling asleep in his arms. What had happened tonight had been wonderful, but she could never ever allow it to happen again.

As much as she loved Jackson and as much as he thought he loved her, she knew once she was completely back on her feet, it was time for her to return to the swamp where she belonged.

If she continued in the relationship, there was no doubt in her mind that he would hurt her. Eventually the novelty of dating a woman from the swamp would wear off. He'd begin to notice the differences between them and not how alike they were. It was possible over time that the peer pressure of the prejudice in town would begin to weigh on him.

He was from the town and there was no doubt in her mind that ultimately he'd go back to the town to find his forever love. A deep sob escaped her and she rolled over to bury her face in the pillow as she began to weep.

For the first time in her life, Josie almost wished she wasn't from the swamp and that only made her cry harder.

Chapter Ten

Jackson awoke early, his thoughts immediately filled with the woman in the other bedroom. Making love with her had been more wonderful than he'd even dreamed. He certainly hadn't expected it to happen last night. She'd been so passionate and giving and he didn't think he could love her any more.

Surely, she loved him, too. Surely, she wouldn't share the intimate act of lovemaking with him if she didn't love him at least a little bit. But he was almost afraid to believe anything about her feelings toward him.

All he could do was be there for her until they caught the man who wanted her dead. There would be time for him to tell her how he felt about her later. With this thought in mind, he got out of bed and hurried into the bathroom for a shower.

Maybe if she was feeling well enough, they'd go to Tremont's for lunch. If there was any man inside the restaurant that she hadn't met at the gala, then he would introduce her to him.

In fact, it would probably be good for them to dine there for lunch and dinner every day. If Josie was right, and it was possible her assailant was from Jackson's social network, then eventually he would show up at Tremont's.

Once he'd showered, he pulled on a pair of black slacks and a short-sleeved black and gray shirt and then he headed for the kitchen. Maybe she'd like some French toast this morning. He had no idea if she liked the dish or not, but he was betting that she did.

The first thing he did was start the coffee brewing and while it worked, he got out the dishes he would need to make the French toast. He also set the table with two plates and the required silverware.

By that time, he was able to pour himself a cup of coffee and then he sank down at the table to wait for her to get up. He liked the look of two plates. He loved having her here in his home with him. She fit. Despite the differences of where they came from, he believed they were meant to be together.

However, once again he was completely confused by her. She'd already confessed she'd only been using him when they first began to see each other. Was she still just using him? There was no question she'd needed somebody after being attacked.

She still wanted to catch her assailant and he was her ticket into the world where she needed to be. Had she made love to him last night just to keep him on the hook?

That thought shot a deep pain through him. He'd

been looking for love for a very long time. He'd always wanted to be married and share his life with a special woman. He'd found that woman in Josie. But was he the man for her? Or was he just a man of convenience for her right now? Was he just a fool?

He shoved these troubling thoughts aside and stared out the nearby window where the sun was just beginning to peek up over the horizon. He still hoped to arrange a night when his buddies could come over to meet Josie. It was Wednesday now—maybe she would feel up to it by Saturday night.

He was halfway through his second cup of coffee when she walked into the kitchen. It was obvious she had just showered. Her hair was still damp and she brought with her the scent of soap and shampoo mingling with the fragrance that was hers alone.

"Good morning," he said and quickly jumped up out of the chair.

"Good morning to you," she replied.

"Have a seat and I'll pour you coffee."

"You're spoiling me, Jackson," she said as he got a cup down from the cabinet and went to the coffee maker.

"You deserve to be spoiled," he replied and set the hot brew in front of her. "I was thinking French toast for breakfast. How does that sound?"

"It sounds delicious."

He was aware of her gaze on him as he started preparing their breakfast. "How did you sleep?" he asked.

"I slept okay. What about you?"

"Like a baby," he replied. He whipped the egg yolks and added milk, wondering if they needed to talk about what they had shared the night before. He decided to wait to see if she brought it up.

Within minutes, breakfast was on the table. While they ate, she was quiet and appeared to be deep in her own thoughts. They were almost finished when he finally broke the silence.

"The bruise on your face is almost gone," he observed.

"Overall, I'm feeling much better and I think it's time for me to go." Her gaze didn't quite meet his.

"Go where?" he asked in surprise.

"Back to my place," she replied.

"Josie, look at me," he said softly, wondering what on earth was going through her mind. Slowly, her dark eyes met his. "Honey, what are you thinking? Somebody is trying to kill you and now isn't the time for you to leave here. I can only thank God that when he encountered you in that parking lot, he didn't have a gun or a knife."

He reached across the table and took one of her hands in his. "In fact, I was just thinking this morning that our next course of action should be to spend lots of time at Tremont's. I believe relatively soon, the man we're looking for will come in there to eat or drink."

He squeezed her hand. "Please don't give up now, Josie. I believe we're so close to finding this guy."

She stared at him for a long moment and then

slowly nodded her head. “Okay, I’ll stay another day or so,” she relented. “Now let me help you clean up the dishes.”

A few more days? Had last night meant absolutely nothing to her? Was she so eager to escape him now that she would prefer to face a killer all alone? Damn, could she confuse him any further?

Don’t get into your head too much, a small voice whispered inside his brain. In the end, he had very little control over the situation…over her.

All he could do at this point was work as hard as he could to introduce her to as many men as possible. He now had about a one-week deadline to catch the man who had tried to kill Josie.

“By the way,” he said as they went into the living room, “I thought since you were feeling better, I’d plan on Saturday night to have my friends over. How do you feel about that?”

“That would be fine,” she replied. She sank down on the sofa and he sat in his chair.

“And how about lunch today at Tremont’s?”

She immediately frowned. “I really don’t have the clothes to go there.”

“Honey, you rock a pair of leggings and any top you put on. You’ll be fine no matter what you wear,” he replied. “Besides, look at it this way, we’re partners and we’re on a secret mission to catch a potential killer.”

“Okay then, I’m in,” she replied.

They agreed on eleven o’clock for lunch and then she excused herself and went into her bedroom. He immediately got on the phone to call his buddies and set up things for Saturday night. He got hold of everyone and it all fell into place. After that, he went into his office to check on emails and updates on several projects he was involved in.

When he was finished with all that, he went back into his bedroom and pulled on his gun holster and gun and then grabbed a lightweight casual sports coat and carried it back into the living room. Once there, he pulled on the sports coat over his gun. He wasn't about to go out in public with Josie without his weapon for defense.

Josie remained in her room until quarter to eleven and then she came back into the living room. She was clad in black leggings and a short-sleeved black and white blouse.

"You look gorgeous, Josie," he said.

"Thank you, but I don't feel very gorgeous right now. I threw this blouse into my suitcase to bring here because it was comfortable, not because it was particularly stylish."

"Well, whatever the reason, it looks very good on you," he replied. A flashback of her naked and on top of him suddenly shot through his mind. It instantly evoked a new desire for her, a reminder of the depth of love he had for her in his heart…in his very soul.

"Shall we go?" he asked. Once again, he had to remind himself that she was the one in control. If she didn't love him, then he would just have to figure out how to live without her.

It was precisely noon when they arrived at the restaurant. He was pleased to see that the parking lot was fairly full. His nerves began to tighten all his muscles.

Was it possible that today would be the day they'd find Josie's attacker? Would it be somebody Jackson had shared drinks with? Would it be somebody he'd sat across a lunch table from?

As they walked in, his gaze went to the bar to see who was sitting there. All six men who occupied the seats there had been at the gala and Josie had already met them.

As the hostess seated them at a two-top toward the back, he checked the diners to see who Josie hadn't yet met. He stopped briefly at a booth where Patrick James and his wife sat.

Patrick was a young guy who worked at the bank. Jackson had done business with him several times in the past and he didn't remember seeing them at the gala. "Hey, Patrick, good to see you," Jackson now said to the man.

"Jackson, good to see you, too," he replied. "You remember my wife, Brianna."

"I do, and this is Josie Cadieux."

"Nice to meet you both," Josie said.

"We missed you at the big gala," Jackson said.

"Yeah, we were sorry to miss it but Brianna wasn't feeling well that night," Patrick said. "But there will be other galas."

"That's for sure. And now we'll just leave you to enjoy your meal," Jackson said.

Moments later, Jackson and Josie were seated. "Not him?" Jackson asked.

"Not him," Josie confirmed. "I'll never forget the sound of his voice." She released a deep sigh. "I feel like we're looking for a needle in a haystack."

"But the haystack is getting smaller and smaller," he replied, wanting to chase the darkness out of her eyes.

"It would help if I believed Gravois was doing a real investigation into everything," she said. "And if he's not interested in my case, then I wish he would do more to catch the swamp monster."

"At least he's looking to hire some new people. Maybe fresh eyes on that case will result in it finally being solved," he replied.

"That would definitely be great. I worry every day that it's just a matter of time before another swamp woman will be killed."

"I hate to tell you this, Josie, but right now all my attention and energy is on you and what's happening in your life," he said.

At that moment, the waitress appeared to take their orders. They both ordered club sandwiches and sweet tea to drink. "Josie, I don't want you to go home until after we catch the guy who tried to kill you," he said once their meals arrived. "I don't care if it takes a week or a month. As long as you're with me, you'll be safe."

"Jackson, you brought me back to your house to heal, and I've done that," she replied.

"That's true, but I also brought you to my house to protect you from harm and I still want to protect you," he stressed. "Josie, please consider staying with me until we catch this guy."

She frowned and dragged one of her French fries through a pool of ketchup on her place. "I'll consider it," she finally said. "But, sooner or later I need to go home. What happens if we never catch this guy?"

"I believe we will," he replied with determination. "If we have to go door-to-door and have each man talk to us so you can recognize his voice, then that's what we'll do."

She smiled at him. "I'm not sure what I did in a previous life to deserve you, Jackson."

"Honestly, Josie, it's just the opposite. You've already changed my life for the positive in so many ways. I look at things so differently because of you and you've made me a much better man."

"This conversation has gotten way too serious for a lunch date," she replied with an uncomfortable laugh.

"You're right. So, let's talk about favorite animals. I'm personally drawn to the aardvark." He knew he'd make her laugh and she did.

From that point on, the conversation was lighter, but as they talked and enjoyed the food, he kept scanning the crowd for men she hadn't met.

They were almost finished eating when Sonny came in. He had Loretta Hannity, his latest in a long string of girlfriends, by his side.

Jackson motioned to him and the two headed toward them. "Josie, this is my buddy, Sonny Landry and his friend Loretta Hannity," he said.

"Josie, it's great to finally meet you," Sonny said. "I've heard so much about you."

"I've heard a lot about you, too," Josie replied with a smile.

"I'm sure it was all lies," Sonny returned with a laugh.

"Loretta, don't let this guy lead you into trouble," Jackson said.

"Don't worry, I'm trying to keep him out of trouble," Loretta said with a small laugh. "Josie, it's nice meeting you," she added.

"You, too," Josie replied.

"I guess we'll see you guys on Saturday night," Sonny said.

"We're looking forward to it," Jackson said.

The two moved on to their seats and Jackson looked at Josie intently. "Not him?" he asked, half holding his breath.

"Not him," she replied.

He released a relieved sigh. The last thing he'd want to find out was that one of his close friends was Josie's monster. The only other man he saw that Josie hadn't met on the night of the gala was dependent on a walker. There was no way he was the man they sought.

"We'll come back for dinner," he said once they were in the car and headed back to his place.

"I intend to pay you back for all the meals out," Josie said. "I have cash at my place to repay you."

"You know I don't care about the money, Josie. I have more money than I'll ever spend in my lifetime. I'm not worried about the cost of eating out."

"I care," she replied. "You should know by now that I pay my own way, Jackson."

"As you wish," he finally said. He had forgotten that she was such a proud woman, something he admired in her.

They got back home and settled in for an afternoon of movie watching. They still hadn't spoken about what had happened between them the night before. It was obvious she didn't feel the need to discuss it. Was that because it had meant nothing to her?

Eventually when she went back home, would they resume the same relationship they'd had before all this happened? Could that even happen? He missed sitting on that fallen tree trunk in the swamp and talking to her about everything and nothing.

Would they be able to go back to that time where they were building their relationship? Could they recapture the innocence of that time in their lives? His worse fear was that she would go back to the swamp and never want to see him again.

JOSIE TRIED TO focus on the comedy movie that was playing on the television, but her head was filled with questions that churned around and around.

Was it really possible that they'd come across her

attacker by dining at Tremont's? Would it…could it be that easy? What if the man didn't eat there? The mission they were on suddenly felt totally futile.

And then there was the fact that she was continuing to lead Jackson on, letting him believe there might be a relationship between them after this was over…if it was ever over.

The absolute worst thing she could have done was make love with him. She'd allowed her desire for him to override her good sense. She was sure it had given him hope that they would be a couple after this was all over. Still, even knowing that, she was glad she'd had the opportunity to share such intimacy with him.

She would keep the memory of him forever in her mind…in her heart. In the evenings when the bullfrogs sang their deep-throated songs and the soft waves of the water rhythmically slapped against the shanty, when a deep loneliness swept through her soul, she would remember the town man who came into the swamp and loved her for a little while.

"I thought we'd head back to Tremont's for dinner about five," Jackson said, breaking the silence that had built up between them.

"This all feels so futile," she replied and turned to look at him. "Jackson, what if he never comes in to Tremont's to eat? What if you're just wasting all this money and time and I'm never able to identify this man?" She was aware her frustration, her anger at the situation was rife in her voice.

"Josie, I know this is all very upsetting to you. But

you promised me, at the very least, that you would give this a week. We're getting together with my friends on Saturday night and after that we'll see where we are and how we move forward, okay?" His gaze caressed her with softness that instantly soothed some of the anger that had momentarily gripped her.

"That gives us tonight, tomorrow and Friday to eat at Tremont's," he continued. "These are the busiest times at the restaurant. So, are you still with me?" This time there was a soft pleading in his eyes.

"Okay, I'm still in," she finally replied. She feared going back home, knowing there was somebody out there who wanted her dead, but she also feared staying here with Jackson and falling deeper and deeper in love with him.

When it was close to when they were leaving for dinner, she went back into her bedroom to change her blouse from the one she'd worn at lunchtime to something different.

When she'd packed to leave the swamp, all that had been on her mind was bringing with her the most comfortable clothing she had. She definitely hadn't thrown in any special blouses for dining out at a fancy restaurant.

She found another top that would be adequate and shook it in an attempt to get most of the wrinkles out. She now believed they were chasing the moon, set on an impossible quest that would only expend their energy and hopes.

Still, she had given Jackson a week or so, and she

would stand by her word. She'd never broken a promise in her life and the last thing she wanted to do was break a promise she'd made to Jackson. But there was no question it would be difficult to continue to stay here with him.

She found herself wanting him again. She wanted his big strong arms to hold her close. She'd never felt as safe as she did with him. When she was in his embrace, all the ugliness of the outside world melted away and there was only him and his soft blue eyes.

One more week and she'd be back in the swamp. At least she knew the man who was after her didn't know the location of her shanty. She'd wait a couple of weeks before she attempted to sell her fish again. She wouldn't venture out of the shanty for a while.

She knew that Jackson would continue to put pressure on Gravois when she was gone, but there was no way they'd find the man without her. If the creep did find her shanty, she'd just have to make sure she was ready to fight for her life.

When she was finished dressing, she returned to the living room where Jackson was waiting for her. He smiled at her…that soft smile that always stirred her on so many levels inside.

"As always, you look positively beautiful," he said.

She frowned and plucked at the front of the blouse. "I don't feel very beautiful. I certainly don't feel like I'm ready to walk into a fancy restaurant for dinner."

"What are you worried about, Josie? That a bunch of bigots might judge you?"

His words made her laugh. "You're right. I don't give a damn about how people talk about me." The laughter died on her lips. "But I do worry on your account."

"Well, don't. I don't give a damn how people talk about me, either." He took her by the arm. "Now, let's go have a nice dinner together."

For some reason, tonight felt different. It felt more like a date than a mission. As they drove there, Jackson kept the conversation light and entertaining, and she found herself relaxing and just enjoying his company.

By the time they were seated at a booth inside the restaurant, some of her tension had returned and twisted tight in the pit of her stomach.

She looked around and recognized most of the men inside. She noticed Jackson gazing at their fellow diners as well. The two men she didn't recognize were too old to have given her the kind of beatdown she'd received. Jackson must have thought they were too old as well for he didn't say anything about introducing them to her.

When the waitress arrived, he ordered the steak and she got the baked fish. Once their meals had been served, their conversation continued to be light and easy, but his gaze on her was intent and filled with a flirtatious sparkle.

As they ate, his gaze also continued to scan the crowd, making her remember the real reason they were here. She prayed they'd find the guy tonight.

Then tomorrow she would be able to return to her life in the swamp before Jackson had ever entered into it.

However, it didn't happen. When they left the restaurant two hours later, a wave of hopelessness swept through her. Once again, she felt as if they were just wasting their time and energy.

"Stop it, Josie," he said softly when they were in the car and headed back to his place.

She looked at him in surprise. "Stop what?"

"Stop doubting the process and falling down into a dark hole," he said.

"How do you know that's what I'm doing?"

He flashed her a quick smile. "Because I know you and I've learned some of your moods. Josie, I know how badly you want to find this man. Okay, so we came up empty-handed today, but I have hope that we'll get him tomorrow."

"Have you always been such a wide-eyed optimist?" she asked curiously.

He hesitated a moment before replying. "I never thought about it before, but yes, I've pretty much always seen the glass half-full. I think that's the way you saw the world before all of this happened to you."

He pulled into the driveway, stopped the engine and then turned in the seat to look at her. "Josie, I desperately want to give your life back to you… the one where you didn't have a worry in the world and didn't have to live looking over your shoulder. I… I want to be the hero in this story. I want to be your hero."

"Oh, Jackson." She reached out and stroked the side of his beautiful face. "You are my hero in so many ways." She dropped her hand. "Never feel like you haven't been my hero."

He slowly nodded and then together they got out of the car and went inside. She sank down on the sofa and he sat in his chair. "Whew, I think I ate too much," she said, hoping to lighten the mood once again.

"Yeah, me, too," he agreed. "But I always eat too much when I go to Tremont's. The food there is very good."

"I know my fish tonight was excellent," she replied.

"So, want to watch a little television before bedtime?" he asked.

"Sure."

Minutes later, they were watching a crime drama that immediately intrigued her. It was good to focus on somebody else's drama for an hour or two instead of being consumed by thoughts of her own.

"I would have sworn the killer was the nephew," she said once the show was over. "It was shocking to find out her own brother killed her."

"Yeah, I was surprised, too. I was leaning toward the boyfriend being the guilty party," Jackson replied.

She grinned at her. "Then that proves it. We both stink at solving a murder."

He laughed. "This just proves that we stink at solving this particular case. I refuse to wear a loser badge over this. Do you want to watch one more and see if we do any better?"

"Sure," she agreed.

He turned on another hour-long crime show and once again she lost herself in the drama playing out on the screen.

She didn't want to think about the fact that a man wanted her dead. She also didn't want to think about the heartache that she knew was in her future where Jackson was concerned.

In just a couple of days, she would leave here and she knew she would probably never see Jackson again.

Chapter Eleven

Jackson was almost as upset as Josie was as they came home from the restaurant on Thursday night. It had been another futile night. He'd introduced her to three more men she hadn't met at the gala, but unfortunately none of them had been the one they sought.

His biggest fear was that she intended to leave his place and her potential killer would still be out there plotting and planning on how he could get close to her, on how he could murder her.

They now sat in his living room, once again watching television. But despite the entertaining comedy that played on the screen, he couldn't keep his gaze away from her.

His love for her positively ached inside him. He knew her plans were probably to leave here and go home on Sunday and he dreaded when that time came.

He couldn't imagine how empty the house would feel, how very empty his life would feel without her in it. But he had known all along that eventually his time with her would run out and she would have to go home. He just didn't want her to go.

He now glanced at her once again. She was clad in a pair of navy leggings and a red and navy blouse. Her hair fell around her shoulders in a veil of silky darkness and he wanted nothing else than to reach out and stroke her beautiful hair.

Still, it was so much more than just her physical beauty he would miss. He would miss her sharp wit and intelligence. He was going to miss their long conversations and shared laughter.

What he hoped was they would continue their relationship when she went home. Her making love with him the other night had given him new hope that they could get through everything and still have a wonderful future together.

His only hope right now was that tomorrow they would identify her attacker. Tremont's was always super busy on Fridays, not so much at lunchtime, but the place rocked with people on Friday evenings.

Surely, her attacker would come in then to eat and socialize. Jackson had made reservations to assure that he and Josie would have a table or booth waiting for them when they arrived.

"I'm looking forward to Saturday night," he said during a commercial.

She turned and smiled at him. "So am I. I'm looking forward to meeting these hooligans you call your best friends."

He laughed. "I'll have you know that we've all grown out of the hooligan days of our past."

"Ha, I'll be the judge of that after Saturday night," she replied.

"Hopefully by Saturday night we will have identified your attacker and all will be well. I have a good feeling about tomorrow night. I think he'll show up for dinner at the restaurant and then Saturday night we'll have a big celebration because he's in jail."

The laughter that had momentarily lit her eyes darkened. "I'd like that but I'm certainly not getting my hopes up too high."

It didn't happen at lunch on Friday and all Jackson could hold onto was the fact that it had to happen at dinner. Josie was quiet Friday afternoon when they got back to the house after lunch.

He didn't know what to say to her to keep her hopes up because he was having trouble holding onto his own. He was desperate to keep her here as long as any danger surrounded her. But he was also aware that she was a strong-minded woman who would do what she wanted and if she wanted to go back to the swamp, then there was absolutely nothing he could do about it.

It was on the local news that another young woman from the swamp had been killed by the murderer that everyone called the Honey Island Swamp Monster.

Her body was found in the alley behind the bank. According to the report, she was stabbed to death and her throat and face were ripped out by a claw of some sort. The injuries were so bad they had yet to make an identification of her.

"Dammit," Jackson said as he hit pause on the television. "I was hoping this wouldn't happen again until Gravois and his team caught the monster."

"Like that's really going to happen," Josie replied derisively. "He's never going to catch anyone for anything."

"I just can't figure out how this murderer is getting away without leaving a single clue behind," he said. "These are obviously heinous crimes with plenty of blood. How is this monster getting away without leaving behind a footprint or something?"

"Who knows," Josie replied.

"I'll give it a couple of days and then I'm going to be all over that man's ass again," Jackson said as a rich anger rocked through him. "He didn't help you when you first went to him, he's done nothing since somebody tried to kill you and now this, another poor woman dead."

"I wonder if he knows who the Honey Island monster is and I also wonder if he knows who's after me."

Jackson looked at her in surprise. "What do you mean? Why would you wonder that?"

She shrugged. "I think both men are from town and I wonder if he's protecting somebody he knows. He's made it pretty clear that he doesn't really care about the people in the swamp."

"I know Gravois is lazy and prejudiced, but I can't

imagine him covering for such a vicious killer as the Honey Island Swamp Monster."

"We may have to agree to disagree on that," she replied. She frowned. "I wonder if I knew her, if she was one of my friends."

"If that's the case, then I'm sorry for your loss," he said softly.

Her comment about Gravois stayed in his mind the remainder of the afternoon. Was it possible that the lawman was covering up for somebody? Maybe one of his wealthy friends? He didn't think a lot of Gravois, but he didn't want to believe the man was capable of that.

Would Gravois allow somebody to kill Josie? Was it possible he knew who attacked her but he didn't want to identify the person because he was a friend of the lawman? If Jackson found out that was true, then he'd not only see the man out of his office, but he'd do everything in his power to see him in jail for a very long time to come.

It was about four o'clock when Josie got up off the sofa. "Do you happen to own an ironing board and iron?" she asked.

"Actually, I do." He got up from his chair. "They're in my bedroom. I'll go get them for you."

"Thanks, the blouse I'm wearing tonight is all wrinkled from being stuffed in the bottom of my bag. It could definitely use the lick of a hot iron."

She stood close to him as he set the board up in her bedroom. As always, her nearness stoked a flame deep inside him. His heartbeat accelerated and all he wanted to do was take her in his arms and repeat what they had shared together before.

He plugged in the iron and then, to leave the room, he had to walk close to her once again. He stopped in front of her, his love burning hot in his lungs and in every fiber of his being.

"Josie, I… I want to kiss you," he said, his voice husky with his desire.

"I… I'd like that," she whispered.

He gathered her into his arms and took her lips with his in a tender kiss that held all the love for her that burned in his heart. She raised her arms around his neck and leaned into him.

It was Josie who deepened the kiss, sneaking her tongue into his mouth to swirl with his. He tightened his arms around her, wanting…needing to hold her close forever.

However, it was also Josie who broke off the kiss and took a step back from him. "Thanks for the iron," she said, her gaze not quite meeting his.

"No problem," he replied, his desire for her still burning hot through his veins.

"I should be ready to go in about half an hour. Does that work?"

"Perfect," he replied. "Then I'll just get out of here and let you get ready."

He left the room and she closed the door after him. He went back into the living room and paced the floor, waiting for some of his sexual tension to pass. He was wound so tight he felt like he might explode. The woman utterly confused him. Her kisses said one thing, but her mouth and actions said something else altogether.

He was surprised when a knock fell on his door. Maybe it was Gravois with some good news for a change. Or maybe it was somebody else with a more nefarious intent. He grabbed his gun from the end table just to be on the safe side and then went to the door.

He looked through his peephole and then unlocked the door and pulled it open. "Hey, buddy, what are you doing here? The party is tomorrow night."

"More importantly, what are you doing? Give me that before you shoot all your toes off." Brian grabbed the gun from Jackson. "And I know the party is tomorrow night, but I stopped by to tell you we can't come. The wife had made plans that she neglected to tell me about until this morning."

"Well, come on in and sit for a few. You can at least meet Josie."

Brian followed him into the living room where he sank down on the sofa and placed the gun on the end table next to him. "So, where is the lady of the hour?"

"She's getting dressed. We're going to Tremont's tonight for dinner." Jackson sat in his chair facing his friend. "It seems like forever since I last saw you. What's up in your life these days?"

"Oh, Cynthia has been keeping me busy around the house. She's decided our place needs a total remodel and she's driving me more than a little bit crazy."

Jackson laughed. "I know Cynthia is hardheaded. She always was. I remember even in high school she ran you around in circles."

"You don't know the half of it," Brian replied with a deep sigh.

"Do you want a drink?" Jackson asked.

"Sure, I wouldn't mind a small shot of whiskey."

Jackson got up from the chair. "Coming right up." He went to the bar and poured the shot and then carried it back to Brian.

"Thanks," Brian replied. "So, how are things going with you? I was sorry to hear about Josie getting beat up. I heard that it was pretty bad."

"Somebody tried to kill her, Brian, and that somebody is still out there somewhere," Jackson said. "That's why she's been staying with me. I'm trying to protect her and keep her alive."

"So, Gravois doesn't have any clue as to who it might have been?" Brian asked.

"Of course, he doesn't. He doesn't know where his own ass is on most days," Jackson replied scornfully. "And now I heard this afternoon on the news that he has another murder on his watch."

"The woman from the swamp, yeah, I heard about it on the morning news." Brian shook his head. "It's too damn bad."

"Yeah, and Gravois is probably sitting on his ass in his office and doing as little as possible about it."

"I heard yesterday he's hired some special private investigator to come in and work on the Honey Island monster murders."

"I hope you're right because somebody needs to be investigating those murders for real," Jackson replied. "If he hired somebody, then it would be the first smart thing he's done since he's been in office."

"You got that right." Brian swallowed his shot and then set the empty glass down on the coffee table.

"Want another?" Jackson asked.

"I'd love one, but I better not. I'm driving and I've got a lot to do when I get back home. Cynthia wants me to take the kids to the park so she can have a little time to herself."

"Well, that should be fun," Jackson replied.

"Yeah, I always enjoy having father time with them."

"I can't wait until I have some kids of my own," Jackson replied.

"I'm sure you'll be a good dad."

Jackson smiled at his friend. "Josie should be out here any minute now. I'm really eager for you to meet her."

Brian returned the smile. "After all the things you've said about her, I'm definitely eager to meet her, too."

The two continued to visit for several more minutes and then heard the sound of the bedroom door opening. Brian stood, as did Jackson as Josie entered the room.

She looked utterly lovely clad in a pair of navy leggings and a tunic-style red blouse. The color emphasized the darkness of her hair, which fell rich and shiny across her shoulders.

Her features radiated surprise that they had a guest, but she offered a friendly smile at Brian. "Josie, this is my good friend Brian Miller," Jackson said. "And Brian, this is Josie Cadieux."

"Nice to officially meet you, Josie," Brian said.

Josie's smile froze on her face as she stared at him. "You," she finally said in a mere whisper.

Jackson looked at her and then gazed back at his good friend in stunned surprise. What? What was happening here? Brian?

"You're the man who raped me…the man who beat me," Josie said, her voice trembling with emotion. "It's him, Jackson. I swear it's him."

"Brian?" Once again, Jackson stared at Brian. Surely, there was some kind of mistake here. Surely, this couldn't be true.

"Oh, Josie. I was so hoping you wouldn't be able to identify me," Brian said. "But this changes everything." He picked up Jackson's gun from the end table and pointed it at her.

JOSIE FELT AS if all the blood had left her body. The moment she heard his voice, she knew with a certainty that it was him. As she stared at the man who had raped her…the man who had nearly beaten her to death and now had Jackson's gun in his hand, icy chills raced up her spine.

"Brian, what in the hell are you doing?" Jackson asked with obvious surprise. "Put the gun down and talk to me."

"Sorry, I can't do that, Jackson," he replied.

"Is this all true? Did you rape Josie? Are you the one who tried to kill her?"

Brian ignored Jackson and instead motioned to Josie. "Move over there next to Jackson," he said.

She didn't move. She couldn't. Her body was frozen in place. Imminent danger snapped in the air and she couldn't even breathe. "Move," Brian yelled. He turned the gun on Jackson. "Move or I shoot him right now."

That snapped the inertia that had momentarily gripped her body. She quickly stepped over to stand next to Jackson. Oh, God, she had brought this danger into his life. What did Brian have in mind? She knew he intended to kill her, but what about Jackson? What did he intend for him?

"Brian, what the hell?" Jackson now said, obviously upset.

"It's all true, Jackson, but it wasn't my fault," Brian said. "Cynthia had been ragging on me all day long and that night I'd had enough. I was filled with an enormous rage and I decided to go to the swamp and take the first woman I found. That woman just happened to be Josie."

She could feel Jackson's rage growing. She felt it

in the tenseness of his body next to hers. She heard it in his heavy, erratic breathing.

"How in the hell did I know you were going to hook up with a piece of swamp trash," Brian continued. "Jackson, I can't let her ruin my life. She'll ruin my marriage and my reputation. I've worked too damn hard and long for it all to be ruined by swamp trash." Once again, Brian's voice was strident.

"You brought her into our world, Jackson, and that was your big mistake. Now I have to take care of both of you."

"What does that even mean, Brian?" Jackson asked. "What do you intend to do now?"

"It will be tragic…a murder/suicide," Brian said, once again making chills shoot through her. "You made it easy for me by handing over your gun to me. It will be the weapon that Josie kills you with and then blows her own brains out. It will be a cautionary tale for men who want to hook up with the swamp and invite that stink into their lives and people will talk about it for years to come."

A murder/suicide? Josie's brain worked hard to wrap around what was happening right now. She stared at Brian in horror. A murder/suicide? That meant he not only intended to kill her, but Jackson as well.

"Brian, think about it. I'm your good friend… one of your very best friends." Jackson took a step toward the man. "We have always had each other's backs. I'll help you get through this. We'll get you the best attorney that money can buy."

Brian laughed, the sound utterly maniacal. "I don't need an attorney because there's only three of us who know about this, and two of us are going to be dead."

"Don't hurt Jackson," Josie said as tears filled her eyes. "Please…he has nothing to do with any of this. He's innocent and he doesn't deserve to die." A deep sob escaped her. Her tears weren't for herself but rather for Jackson, who had only been good and loving toward her.

"Kill me, but please leave him alone," she continued frantically. "Shoot me, you can tell the police it was an accident. Jackson will cover for you, he's one of your best friends."

"You stupid whore, he's crazy in love with you. He's not going to cover for me," Brian half shouted. His face was red and sweat had begun to shine on his forehead.

"So, what's your plan, Brian?" Jackson asked, his voice surprisingly cool and calm in the madness that surrounded them. "Are you going to shoot me first, or Josie first?" Jackson took another step closer to the gunman. "How exactly is this going to go down? You might be many things, Brian, but you aren't a cold-blooded killer."

"Yes, I am," Brian replied. "You have no idea what I'm capable of. I enjoyed beating her, Jackson. I enjoyed hitting and kicking her as hard as I could."

At that moment, Jackson launched himself toward Brian. He smashed into Brian's chest. The gun fired off as the two men fell to the floor.

Josie screamed and, as the gun skittered across the floor, she picked it up. "Stop it," she shrieked. When the men continued to grapple with each other, she fired the gun into the ground.

Both men stopped fighting. Brian got to his feet and Jackson rose to his knees. "Watch him, Josie," Jackson said as he did a quick pat down of Brian. He found Brian's gun in his pocket and tossed it so it slid across the floor and landed at Josie's feet.

She kicked it behind her, her sole focus on the man who had stolen what wasn't his to take from her. She was vaguely aware of Jackson sitting back down on the floor and taking his cell phone from his pocket.

"You don't want to shoot me, Josie," Brian said smoothly as he took a small step toward her. "You aren't a killer."

"Stay where you are," she warned. "You have no idea what I'm capable of," she said, throwing his words back at him. "I promise you, there's nothing more I'd like to do than shoot you for all you've done to me."

Her eyes narrowed and it was just her and the man who had tried to kill her. "If I could, I would stomp on your head and kick you in the ribs until they all broke, but since I can't do all that, I'd be more than happy to shoot you."

For the first time since she'd entered the living

room, Brian looked afraid. "Josie, the police are on their way." Jackson's voice filtered through to her brain.

"As slow as Gravois is, I still have time to kill him," she replied.

"Please...please don't," Brian said as he raised his arms up in the air in surrender. "Please, Josie, I... I have two small children."

"You were going to kill us and then take them to a playground to play. You're sick, Brian," Jackson said.

"Were you thinking of your children when you dropped that bag over my head? Were you thinking of them when you pushed me down to the ground?" she half screamed as she remembered all the details of the assault.

"Please, I'm sorry. I'm so sorry about everything," Brian replied with a whimper. "I told you it wasn't my fault. It just...just happened. Please, Josie, don't shoot me."

The sound of sirens filled the air. Myriad emotions raced through her. He disgusted her. Just looking at him made her feel sick to her stomach.

There was a part of her that wanted to kill him, but there was a saner part of her that knew he'd be facing his own living hell in the weeks and months to come.

Within minutes, Gravois and two of his officers burst into the townhouse. He stopped short and looked at the scene.

"Thank God you're here," Brian exclaimed. "They

called me over here and accused me of raping Josie and trying to beat her up, but it wasn't me." He pointed a finger at Josie. "That crazy bitch is threatening to kill me."

"He did it," Josie said. "He did it, Gravois, and he came here to kill us so nobody would ever know it was him, so nobody would tell the truth about him."

"Gravois, what Josie says is true," Jackson said from his seat on the floor. "He came here to kill us and he shot me with my own damn gun. Arrest him, Gravois. He's a rapist and an attempted murderer."

As Jackson's words filtered through her overworked brain, she shot him a surprised look and suddenly noticed a pool of blood coming from a wound someplace on his left side. He'd been shot? Oh, God, Jackson had been shot?

She couldn't tell exactly where he'd been shot and where all the blood was coming from, but the sight of it terrified her.

"Oh, Jackson," she cried. Her heart squeezed so tight she could scarcely breathe. "Get an ambulance," she shouted. She handed the gun to Gravois and then ran to Jackson's side and began to cry in earnest.

"How bad is it?" she asked amid her sobs. "I'm sorry, Jackson. I'm so sorry. I never meant for you to get hurt. This wasn't supposed to happen."

"I know that, honey." He smiled at her, but she saw the pain deep in his eyes. She took his hand in hers and squeezed it tight. He looked over to where Gravois was placing Brian in handcuffs.

"They're both lying," Brian yelled. "They're both crazy. Listen to me, Gravois."

"You can tell it to the judge," Gravois replied. With Brian handcuffed, he nodded to one of the patrolmen. "Take him out and lock him in the backseat of my car."

"Just let me go," Brian appealed. "Please, I'm innocent. They're both lying. You'll be sorry about this, Gravois. I have a lot of money and power in this town."

"You'll have nothing when this news gets out," Jackson replied in obvious disgust.

Brian continued to profess his innocence as he was led out of Jackson's house. By that time, the ambulance had arrived and two paramedics pushed in a gurney.

Josie's head was still spinning and she continued to cry as they loaded up Jackson and swept him away. She wanted to go with him to find out how badly he was wounded, but Gravois told her she needed to stay there to be questioned.

An hour or so later, she had told the lawman everything that had occurred from the moment she had recognized Brian's voice. Afterward, Gravois agreed to take her to the hospital where he also needed to find out about Jackson's gunshot wound. Although more than anything she wanted to get to Jackson, she also wanted to give Gravois all the information he needed to keep Brian under arrest.

Once she was in Gravois's car, all her thoughts about Jackson filled her head. Had Brian halfway succeeded in his plan? Had Jackson's gunshot wound been a fatal one? Once again, her heart constricted so much she could scarcely draw a breath.

Jackson couldn't die. She prayed that he was going to be okay. If he did die, then his death was on her hands. First of all, she'd used him and then she'd invited danger and death into his life. Oh, God, he couldn't die.

When they reached the hospital, she bolted from the car and hurried inside to the emergency room desk. "Jackson Fortier," she blurted out. "He was just brought in with a gunshot wound. I… I need to talk to somebody. I need to know how he's doing."

"And you are?" the nurse at the desk asked.

"Josie… Josephine Cadieux," she said.

Gravois came up behind her. "And I need to speak to the doctor in charge of his case."

"I'll let the doctor know you are both here," she replied. She stood and disappeared through a doorway. She returned only moments later. "He said for you both to have a seat and he'll be out when he can."

Josie turned and then sank down in one of the green plastic chairs. Gravois sat down next to her. "I never would have believed this of Brian. He's always appeared to be a fine, upstanding family man."

"I guess you can never know what's in the minds and hearts of people," she replied.

"Why didn't you shoot him?" Gravois asked curiously. "You had the gun in your hand. Before we arrived, why didn't you just pop him one?"

"Trust me, I thought about it long and hard. But first of all, it would be me stooping down to his level and second of all, his death by my hands would have been a deep stain on my very soul."

They fell silent after that. The minutes ticked by agonizingly slow. What was taking so long? Oh, God, how badly had he been hurt? She didn't even know where the bullet had hit him. Had it hit his heart? His lungs? Had it been a deadly shot?

She leaned her head back and once again prayed that he was going to be all right. It was about an hour later when Dr. Etienne Richards came out to speak to them.

Josie jumped out of her chair. "How is he?"

"He was very lucky. The bullet traveled in and out of his upper outer thigh. It was a clean shot that involved no further muscle damage. I've got it cleaned up and stitched and I've given him some pain meds. I intend to keep him for the night but, barring any complications, he should go home tomorrow."

Josie released a shuddery sigh of relief. Thank God it hadn't been worse. Thank God he was going to be just fine.

"Can I see him?" Gravois asked.

Etienne frowned. "I gave him enough pain meds to let him sleep. Can't your questions wait until tomorrow morning?"

"I suppose they can," Gravois said. "I'll be back in the morning."

"Can you do me a favor?" Josie asked the lawman.

"What's that?" he asked.

"Can you take me to Vincent's parking lot?"

"I suppose I can do that," he replied.

"I would really appreciate it." Minutes later, she was in the passenger seat of his patrol car and headed to Vincent's.

It was over. Finally, her bogeyman had finally been caught and she was no longer in any danger. It was all over. Jackson was going to be fine and now it was time for her to end it all.

The kindest thing she could do for Jackson was disappear from his life. He could then find a woman from his social standing to marry.

Yes, it was time for her to leave him. It was time she went back to the swamp where she belonged.

Chapter Twelve

Jackson opened his eyes, momentarily disoriented as to where he was and what the time was. As he looked around his surroundings, it all came rushing back to him.

He remembered everything that had happened with Brian. Brian… He still couldn't believe his good friend had shown up at his house with the intent of killing both him and Josie. He couldn't believe he was responsible for everything that had happened to her.

Brian's betrayal stung deeply. He'd known him since they were boys. When had his friend turned into a monster? When had Brian become capable of all the things he had done?

For God's sake, he'd plotted a murder/suicide when he came to Jackson's house. And Jackson had made it half easy for him by allowing Brian to get a hold of his gun.

Thank God things had gone down as they had and Jackson had come out of it with only a wound to his thigh. Hopefully, Brian would go to prison for a very long time for all the crimes he'd committed and the ones he'd intended to commit.

Josie. Where was she right now? He hoped she was at his place, waiting for him to come home. She was free now…free of any fear, free of all the danger. They could now have a life not looking over their shoulders. Hopefully, she'd tell him she was in love with him and they could plan a future together.

He moved his leg and winced as pain shot through him. Thankfully, the bullet had gone in his thigh and not through his heart. He knew he had taken a chance in rushing at Brian, but there had been no way he was going to allow the man to harm Josie. Brian crowing about how much he'd enjoyed beating Josie had been the catalyst that shot an uncontrollable anger through Jackson and he'd made his move.

He'd only been awake a little while when an older woman pushed a cart in with his breakfast. He was happy to see it since he'd missed dinner the night before.

He turned on the television and then ate the scrambled eggs and bacon that was on the plate. He sipped his coffee and had just eaten a cup of fruit when Etienne walked in.

"Ah, my friend, you look much better this morning than you did last night," he said.

Jackson grinned at him. "I'm definitely feeling better this morning except my thigh is hurting me pretty good."

"That's going to hurt for the next couple of days

or so, but hopefully you're a quick healer and it won't bother you for too long."

"So, what's the plan? Can I get out of here?"

"Give us a few minutes to get your discharge papers ready and then you can go. But before that happens, let me change the dressing on your thigh and explain some wound care to you," Etienne said.

An hour later, Jackson was dressed and sat on the edge of the bed, waiting for Sonny to pick him up and take him home. He was eager to get home to Josie. He only wished she had a cell phone. More than anything, he just wanted to hear the sound of her voice. He wanted to hear her with no fear in her tone. He was eager to see her with a bright, happy smile on her face.

Minutes later, Sonny walked in. "What the hell, man?" he said as Jackson stood up from the bed. "I leave you alone for a few minutes and you go and get yourself shot. I already heard a lot of rumors this morning so I need you to fill me in on all the real details."

"I'll fill you in on the way to my place," Jackson replied. His thigh burned and hurt as he walked out of the hospital to Sonny's car in the parking lot, but he was definitely glad to be alive.

Once in the car, he told Sonny everything. He explained about Brian raping Josie and that it was Brian who had beat her up. Finally, he told Sonny about the confrontation that had taken place in his house the night before.

"I heard he'd been arrested, but I had no idea for what. God, it's all so hard to believe," Sonny said. "I mean, I thought I knew Brian."

"Yeah, that makes two of us, but he obviously had some inner demons that none of us knew about or saw," Jackson replied. "He came to kill me, Sonny. He was prepared to kill both me and Josie in some crazy suicide/murder plot."

"I still find it hard to believe. This is definitely going to rock the whole town," Sonny said.

"I know. I feel bad for Cynthia and the children. Unfortunately, they're also victims in this," Jackson replied.

Sonny pulled into his driveway. "Do you need anything? I could make a run to the store for you if you need something."

"No, I'm good. I've got a script for pain pills, but I don't intend to get it filled unless I really need to. But I do appreciate the ride home." Jackson opened the car door.

"No problem. Don't hesitate to call me if you need anything," Sonny said.

"Thanks, Sonny," Jackson said, now eager to get inside and see Josie. He got out of the car and Sonny backed out of the driveway and zoomed down the street.

Slowly, Jackson walked to his front door. It was unlocked. "Honey, I'm home," he said as he walked in.

There was no greeting in reply. "Josie?" He walked into the living room, but she wasn't there.

He walked back to the bedroom, but she wasn't there, either.

She wasn't any place in the house. He sank down in his chair and listened to the silence that surrounded him. Surely, she'd be back. Her bag and clothes were still in the bedroom.

Maybe she'd just taken a walk and would be back soon.

He'd been home about an hour when there was a knock on the door. It was Gravois. "Sorry to bother you but I need to get a full statement from you about what happened here last night," he said.

Jackson ushered him in and the two men sat. "Mind if I record this?" Gravois asked and placed his phone on the coffee table.

"No, I don't mind at all," Jackson said. He would do whatever was necessary to see to it that Brian went to prison for his crimes against Josie.

It took about half an hour to get through the night's events. Gravois occasionally asked a question to make sure the record was clear.

"Well, your story and Josie's are the exact same," the lawman said when they were finished.

"That's because we're both telling the truth about Brian and what happened. By the way," Jackson said as he walked the man back to his front door, "did you ever identify the new victim in the swamp murders yet?"

"Yeah, her name is Lisa Choate. She was twenty-two years old and worked as a housekeeper for May

Welles. And don't worry, I just hired some hotshot investigator from Shreveport. His name is Nick Cain and he comes with great credentials and he is supposed to be here in two weeks' time."

"That's good. Maybe a set of fresh eyes will solve the cases." It was the kindest thing for Jackson to say rather than saying Gravois's lazy ass wasn't working too hard for a solve. "By the way, what happened to Josie when I was taken to the hospital? I'm assuming you saw her after I was taken away by the ambulance."

"She rode to the hospital with me and we spoke to the doctor to make sure you were okay and then she asked me if I would drop her off at Vincent's, so I did. I haven't seen her since then."

Jackson's heart fell. So, she'd gone back to the swamp. He told Gravois goodbye and the lawman left. When he was gone, Jackson returned to his chair.

He couldn't believe that she hadn't waited until he was home. He couldn't believe she'd left without a goodbye to him. What did it mean? Surely, she meant to come back here. At the very least she'd need to come back for her things.

He hadn't yet told her he loved her. He'd had so many chances to tell her, but ultimately he hadn't. There were so many things left unsaid between them. All he could do now was sit and wait to see if she returned.

However, three days later she still hadn't come

back and the desire to see her, to speak to her became all-consuming to him. He couldn't believe she hadn't come by to see how he was doing. He couldn't believe she had left without even saying goodbye to him.

Finally, on the fourth day and with his thigh feeling a little bit better, he drove out to Vincent's and parked.

He got out of his car and headed into the swamp. He really didn't know how to get to her shanty, but he made his way to their tree trunk and sank down.

The fragrance of the swamp surrounded him, reminding him of her. He hoped she'd come by. He felt as if he were in withdrawal, needing a hit of Josie to make him feel better.

However, she didn't come that day, nor the day after and not the day after that. He sat on the trunk for hours each day, hoping and praying he'd see her again.

Finally, on the fifth day, she appeared. She stopped dead in her tracks at the sight of him. "Jackson, what are you doing here?"

"I've been here for the past four days, hoping to see you. Please, Josie. Come sit and talk to me," he replied.

Her reluctance was obvious as she moved slowly and finally sank down next to him. He felt her body heat and smelled the familiar scent of her and all his love buoyed up inside him.

"How's your leg?" she asked.

"Healing up nicely. How have you been doing?" There were so many things he wanted to say to her, but he didn't even know where to begin.

"I'm doing okay," she replied. "The fishing has been great lately."

"That's good." A long moment of tense silence rose up. "Josie, were you not going to tell me goodbye?" he finally asked.

She released a deep sigh. "Oh, Jackson, I thought it was better this way. I figured it was time for you to get back to your life and for me to get back to mine. I just thought it was best if I ripped the bandage off and left."

"But I want you in my life every day and always." He gazed deep into her eyes. "Josie, I'm so in love with you."

She immediately looked away. "Jackson, go back to town and find a nice town woman to love."

"Why on earth would I want to do that? I don't want a nice town woman to love." He thought about the kiss they had shared the day they'd last been together, right before Brian had shown up. "I want you, Josie. I love you and I think if you look deep in your heart, you love me, too."

She looked down at the ground. "I'm sorry, but that just isn't true," she replied softly. "Jackson, I'm very grateful to you, but...but that's all."

"Josie, look me in the eyes and tell me that's not true. Look me directly in the eyes and tell me you aren't in love with me."

Slowly, she raised her gaze to meet his. There was pain in the depths of her beautiful eyes. "It really doesn't matter how I feel. Don't you see? Jackson, it would never work between us."

"Why wouldn't it? Josie, there is absolutely nothing standing in our way now. You're out of danger and now we can fully pursue a relationship together."

He reached out and took her hand in his. "Josie, I'll never love a woman as much as I love you. I want to marry you. I want you to have my babies and build a family with me."

She closed her eyes and tears trembled on the tips of her long dark lashes. "Jackson, don't you get it?" She opened her eyes and the tears trekked down her cheeks. "You're town and town men don't marry swamp. We're fun dalliances for them. We're exotic playthings, but we definitely aren't marriage material."

He stared at her for a long moment. "Oh, this is rich. You talk about how prejudice the townspeople are, but you're the one prejudice against town men."

"I… That's no-not true," she sputtered.

"But it is true. You've just painted a whole group of people that includes me with the same brush. I don't know what all town men are like, but I'm me and I know what I want. I don't give a damn about town or swamp. That has nothing to do with who we are at our core. Love is what matters."

"Jackson, I'm so afraid that in the end you'll hurt me. I'm afraid you'll realize I'm not enough, that I'll never be enough for you. I love you so much but I don't want to get hurt," she replied.

"Say that again," he said softly.

"Say what again? That I'm afraid?"

"No, the other part. The part where you love me so much." Her words filled him with an enormous joy.

"Jackson, I do love you."

"Then, Josie, don't be afraid. Trust me when I say I want you… I need you in my life forever. Hell, woman, I took a bullet for you. What more could you want from me?" he asked teasingly.

"That's not funny, Jackson. I was so scared that night when I realized you'd been shot." Once again, tears filled her eyes.

"Don't cry, Josie. It's all over and we're both alive and now all I want to know is if you'll be with me forever."

She frowned. "But how would this even work? Jackson, you know the swamp is in my very soul."

"I know that," he assured her. "What I envision is that we have the best of both worlds. We work it out like Peyton and Beau have. We spend a week or so in the shanty and then a week or so at our townhome. We can figure it out, Josie. Just give me a chance, please give us a chance."

She stared at him for several long moments. "Okay," she whispered softly.

"Really?"

"Really," she replied. "I love you, Jackson and you have proven to me over and over again what kind of a decent man you are. I'm… I'm willing to take a chance on us."

He stood and pulled her up to a standing position in front of him. Her eyes were now clear and shiny and this time in the depths of them he saw his forever.

"Can I kiss you, Josie?"

"I'll be mad at you if you don't," she replied.

He wrapped his arms around her and pulled her close against him. She came willingly and he took her lips with his. The kiss was deep and filled with emotion.

He tasted her passion but more importantly, he tasted her love for him. It reached inside him and filled up his heart and his very soul. He would spend the rest of his life loving Josie and he would make sure that every day she knew how very much he loved her.

They weren't town and swamp. They were just two people in love. The kiss ended and he smiled at her. "So, how soon are you going to marry me?"

She laughed. "How soon do you want to marry me?"

"Today…last week," he replied.

She laughed again. "You might give me time to wash my hair. I'm only planning to marry once so I want to look my best."

"Seriously, how about we plan a small wedding in about a month."

She released an audible sigh. "That sounds perfect to me because I don't have much when it comes to friends and family," she replied. "But I wouldn't want to cheat your parents out of the wedding they want for their son."

"Okay, then we'll have the wedding in a month and a week," he replied. "And I was thinking, maybe we should get a pet before we start having babies. How about we start with a baby aardvark?" he said.

Her laughter would forever be the music in his life. Her happiness would be the chords that rang melodically in his head forever. He kissed her again and he knew they were going to have a wonderful future together filled with laughter and love.

Epilogue

Josie sat next to Jackson on the bank, their fishing poles in the water before them and his arm around her shoulder. It had been a little over a week since they had professed their love to each other, eight glorious days of spending time with him in the swamp. Tomorrow they would return to the townhouse and spend about two weeks there.

Josie had never been as happy as she was now. Over the past days, they had talked about and planned their future together and during the nights they had made sweet, passionate love.

Brian had been charged with a handful of crimes and the judge had remanded him without bail. Brian had a lawyer who was working on overturning that, but it wasn't a high-dollar attorney that everyone had assumed he would get.

The gossip on the street was that Brian was completely broke. Many of his businesses had failed and he and his family had been, in recent months, living on credit cards.

However, Brian was the furthest thing on Josie's mind today. Josie couldn't believe she had intended to deny herself the pleasure of loving and being loved by Jackson.

The real turnaround for her had been the moment when Jackson accused her of being prejudice against all town men. He had been right. She had allowed Gentry's betrayal of her to paint all the men with the same heartless color.

There was no fear in her heart now. She didn't fear Brian anymore but most importantly, she didn't fear Jackson's love anymore.

"That new guy is supposed to show up any day now to start working for Gravois," he now said.

"I hope he's as good as Gravois has said he is," she replied.

"I'm hoping he can really dig into the monster murders and find the person responsible."

"That makes two of us," she replied. "It's past time the monster was caught."

"Oh…speaking of monsters… I've got one," he exclaimed and jumped to his feet.

"Set the hook, honey," she said and laughed as he reeled as fast and furiously as he could.

He finally got the catfish up on the bank. He looked at her with a boyish excitement. "He's a good one, isn't he? He's the biggest one I've ever caught, right?"

"Yes, he's a good one," she replied with a laugh. She got up and watched as he set his pole to the side and then took the fish off the hook and tossed it into the basket in the water. They planned to sell the fish they'd gathered through the week tonight, before returning to the townhouse tomorrow.

When he was finished with the fish, she wrapped her arms around his neck and he immediately drew her close to him. "You're becoming quite a fine fisherman, Mr. Fancy Pants," she said.

He grinned down at her. "I wouldn't be interested in fishing without my beautiful fishing partner next to me."

"I appreciate that you come fishing with me," she replied.

"Don't you get it yet, Josie? For the rest of our lives, I'll go anywhere you want, I'll do whatever you want because I love you so very much." His gorgeous blue eyes bathed her with his love. "Can I kiss you, Josie?" he asked teasingly.

"I'll be sad if you don't," she replied.

"Since I never want you to be sad..." He took her lips in a tender kiss that spoke of his love and devotion to her.

She knew deep inside her soul that their love was going to last a lifetime. She thanked the stars above for sending her Jackson. She couldn't wait to have his babies and build a forever life with him.

* * * * *

SPECIAL EXCERPT FROM

HARLEQUIN
INTRIGUE

He and his K-9 always get the job done.
But this case will test even the toughest heart.

Military contractor Cash Meyers and his Rottweiler, Bear, show up in time to save Elena Navarro from being abducted by a drug cartel. But they're too late to protect her little brother. Rescuing the boy means confronting a criminal who will sacrifice anything—and *anyone*—to claim Elena. Cash's instincts are battle-honed, but will his intense attraction to Elena put them both in danger?

Read on for a sneak preview of
K-9 Security *by Nichole Severn*

Chapter One

"It's going to be okay." Elena Navarro tried to keep her voice low. It was hard to make sure her brother had heard her over the screams penetrating the windows and doors.

Another burst of gunfire contracted every muscle she owned around Daniel's small frame. She clamped a hand over his mouth to muffle his sobs. They'd hidden beneath their parents' bed, but there was no sign that her mom and dad were ever coming back. "I've got you. I'm not going to let anything happen to you. Okay?"

Daniel nodded, the back of his head pressed against her chest.

Alpine Valley was supposed to be safe. With only two hundred and fifty people in town, the cartel that'd slowly started consuming New Mexico shouldn't have even glanced in their direction. They should've been left alone. Instead, *Sangre por Sangre* had come for blood and recruits.

And Daniel was the prime age to get their attention.

She had to get him out of here. Had to get him somewhere safe.

"Listen to me. If we stay here, they will take you. I need you to do exactly what I say, and we'll be okay." Elena kept her gaze on the closed bedroom door while backing out from underneath the bed, her hand never leaving her brother's side. Carpet burned against her oversensitive skin, but it was nothing compared to the realization that her parents were most likely dead. "Come on."

He didn't move.

"Daniel, come on. We've got to leave." They didn't have much time. The cartel soldiers would start searching homes to make sure they hadn't left anyone behind. By then, it'd be too late. "Let's go."

"Quiero mama." I want mama. He shook his head. "I don't want to leave."

She didn't have time for this. They didn't have time for this. Elena fisted her brother's shirt and dragged him out from beneath the bed. His protests filled the room, and she struggled to get his flailing punches and kicks under control. He didn't understand. He was too young to know what the cartel would do to him if they got their hands on him. "*Para.* We have to go."

Hiking Daniel onto her hip with one arm, she quieted his cries with her free hand. She hugged him to her, his bare feet nearly dragging against the floor. She wasn't tall in any sense of the word, and Daniel had shot up like a beanstalk over the past years.

He was heavy and awkward, but she was all he had left. She'd do whatever it took to get him out of here.

A flashlight beam skimmed over the single window of her parents' bedroom. Elena launched herself against the wall to avoid being seen. The jerking movement dislodged Daniel's black and red unicorn dragon, and he cried out for it.

The beam centered on the window.

"Shh. Shh." Her breath stalled in her chest. Time distorted, seconds seemed like an eternity, and she couldn't seem to keep track of what must have been only an instant. That beam refused to move on. The sound of gunfire had quieted. All she could hear was Daniel's soft cries, but no matter how hard she held on to him, it didn't comfort him.

Shouts pierced through the panes. "I can hear you in there."

The flashlight arced upward. A split second before the window shattered.

Daniel's scream filled her ears.

They didn't have any other choice. They had to run.

Elena hauled him against her chest and pumped her legs as hard as she could. Glass cut through her heel, but she couldn't stop.

"Dragon!" Her brother's sobs intensified as he locked his feet to the small of her back, trying to wiggle free.

"We've got to go!" She ran down the hallway and headed for the front door. It burst open within feet of her reaching it. A dark outline solidified in the doorway. The soldier's flashlight blinded her, but she kept moving. The back door. She just had to get through the kitchen.

"Where do you think you're going?" Heavy footsteps registered from behind.

Her fingers dug into her brother's soft legs as she raced across old yellow decorative tile. They nearly collided with the sliding glass door. Elena clenched the handle to wrench it open.

It wouldn't move.

Panic infused her every nerve ending. The broomstick. Her parents had always laid a broomstick in the door's track to deter break-ins. The flashlight beam gleamed off the reflective glass behind her.

"Nowhere to go, *señorita*," a low voice said. "And what do we have here? Daniel, right? That must make you Elena. Such a pretty name. Your parents are just outside. Give me the boy, and I will take you to them. Easy."

Easy? No. Her instincts told her every word out of his mouth was a lie. Elena turned to face the shadowed soldier, the light mounted on his gun too bright. She pressed her shoulders into the glass door and crouched. Her thighs burned as she tried to support Daniel's weight. "It's going to be okay," she told him.

"That's right." The shadow moved closer. "You know you can't win. Give me the boy. He'll make a fine soldier."

"Over my dead body." She found the thick broomstick with the broken handle. She swung it into the soldier's shin with everything she had.

His scream punctured through the roaring burst of gunfire. Flashes of light gave her enough direction to grab for the door handle, and she and Daniel fled into the backyard. Echoing shouts and pops of bullets closed in. She hiked Daniel higher up her front, his sobs louder now. They couldn't take her car. The cartel would have already set up roadblocks. Their only choice was the desert. Alone. Without supplies. "We're going to make it. We're going to make it."

She wasn't sure if she'd meant that for Daniel or herself.

"You're going to pay for that!" The soldier who'd cornered them in the kitchen tossed the broomstick onto the back patio. His beam scanned the opposite end of the yard, buying her and Daniel mere seconds.

Elena pried a section of chain link fence free from the neighbor's cinder block wall. The opening wasn't big enough for both of them. She maneuvered Daniel through. "Go. Run, and don't stop. Don't look back. I'm right behind you."

"Come with me, Lena. Come on. You can fit." Another sob escaped him. He tugged at her hand to drag her through after him.

She shoved at him through the fence while trying to make the opening large enough to fit her, but it wouldn't budge. "Daniel, go!"

The beam centered on her from the back door. Another burst of gunfire caused cinder block dust and chunks to rain down from above. She ducked to protect her head as though her hands could stop a bullet. "Run!"

Her brother ran.

Movement penetrated her peripheral vision. Followed by pain.

A strong hand fisted a chunk of her hair and thrust her face-first into the wall. Lightning struck behind her eyes. Her legs collapsed from beneath her, but the soldier wouldn't let her fall. He pulled her against him. "You've got more fight in you than I expected. I like that. After we find your brother, I'll come back for you."

"No." A wave of dizziness warped his features. She couldn't make out anything distinctive, but his voice… She'd never forget that voice. The ground rushed up to meet her. Rocks sliced into the back of her head and arms. The shadow was moving to climb the fence as she tried to press herself upright. Daniel. He was going after Daniel. "You can't have him."

Her head cleared enough that she shot to her feet. She jumped the soldier as he tossed his weapon over the fence to the other side. She locked her arms around his throat and held on for dear life. She didn't know how to fight. That didn't matter. She'd do anything to stop these men from getting hold of her brother.

"Get off." Those same strong hands that'd rammed her face into the wall grabbed for her T-shirt and ripped her from his back. Air lodged in her chest as she hit the ground. A fist rocketed into the side of her face, and her head snapped back. "When will you people learn? You're not strong enough to fight us." He grabbed her collar and hauled her upper body off the ground, ready to strike again. "We are everywhere. We are everything."

She couldn't stop the wracking cry escaping up her throat as she cradled one side of her face. She spread her hand into the rock-scaping her parents had put in a few years ago. Her fingers brushed the edge of a fist-size rock. Securing it in her hand, Elena slammed it into the side of his head as hard as she could.

The soldier dropped on top of her. Tears flooded down her face as she tried to get herself under control. She shoved him off, relief and adrenaline fusing into a deadly combination. This wasn't over. The man who'd come after her and Daniel was just one of many. There would be more soon. She had to go. "Daniel."

Elena clawed out from beneath the man's weight and stumbled toward the fence. She managed to squeeze through, but not without the sharp fingers of steel leaving their mark across her neck and chest. Darkness waited on the other side. No sign of movement. No sign of her brother.

She tested the sting at one corner of her mouth with the back of her hand and started jogging. Dead, expansive land stretched out in front of her. Only peppered with Joshua trees, cacti and scrub brush, the desert made it hard to tell where the sky ended and the earth began. And Daniel was out here alone.

"Lena!" His cry forced ice through her veins. Not from ahead as she'd expected. From behind. "Help me! Lena! Let me go!"

Elena turned back to the house. "No. No, no, no—No!"

Brake lights illuminated the sidewalk in front of her parents' house enough for her to get a look at two men forcing her brother into the cargo area of a sleek, black SUV.

"Daniel!" She lunged for the fence she'd just climbed through. Her bare feet slipped in the panic to get back over as fast as possible. She was on the edge of getting to the other side when her body failed her. She fell beside the soldier she'd knocked unconscious. Pain exploded down her arm and into her ribs. It wouldn't stop her.

Daniel's screams died as the cargo lid closed him inside the car.

"No!" This wasn't real. She ran as fast as her body allowed, along the side of the house and toward the front. "Daniel!"

She reached the corner of the house as the car sped away.

The butt of a gun slammed into the side of her head.

And the world went black.

CASH MEYERS GAVE a high-pitched whistle, and his Rottweiler, Bear, launched at the gunman.

Her teeth sank deep into the bastard's arm as the woman the soldier had knocked unconscious hit the ground. A scream echoed through the night, but it was nothing compared to those he'd heard on the way in. Of pain, loss. Of fear. Fires burned out of control from at least three homes that were torched during the recruiting party. *Sangre por Sangre* had raided a small New Mexican town for new blood. And left nothing but devastation.

Bear brought down her target, and Cash called her off with a lower-pitched whistle. His weapon weighed heavy in his hand as he approached the gunman and took aim. "How many others?"

A low laugh was all the answer he received, but Bear's low growl put an end to that. "Too many for you, *mercenario*." Mercenary.

Cash had been called much worse, but the truth was he and the men and women of Socorro Security were the only ones stopping the cartel from gaining utter control of this area. So he'd take it as a compliment. "It's sweet you're concerned about me, but I've got Bear. Who has your back?"

Nervous energy contorted the soldier's expression in the gleam of flames and moonlight. The man's fingers splayed across the dark steel of his automatic rifle. An upgrade from the last time Cash had a run-in with the cartel. "You'll need more than a dog to protect you if you kill me."

"Oh, I'm not going to kill you." He rammed the butt of his weapon into the soldier's head and knocked him out cold. "You're just not going to be happy when you wake up."

"Steh," he told Bear in German. She huffed confirmation as Cash tossed the soldier's gun out of reach and turned his attention to the woman who'd run headfirst into the weapon's stock. Her face came dangerously close to being impaled by one of the cactuses, and he maneuvered her chin toward him. Scratches clawed across her neck while swelling and a split lip distorted sharp cheekbones and smooth skin. She'd fought. That much was clear. He set one hand on her shoulder and shook her. "Hey, can you hear me?"

No answer.

Hell, he should've hit the bastard who'd struck her harder. Or let Bear get her pound of flesh. Cash scanned the street. Sirens pierced through the roar of flames and cries. Not even Bear's low whimper compared to the dread pooled at the base of Cash's spine. He'd been too late. He hadn't seen this coming, and now the people in Alpine Valley had paid the price.

Fire and Rescue rolled up to the burning house across the street. One ambulance in tow. It wasn't enough to treat the people gathering for medical attention. Older couples holding their heads, a man calling a woman's name, a toddler screaming in his mother's arms.

Sangre por Sangre had ruined lives tonight.

Because of him.

"Daniel." The woman at his feet cracked her eyes

open. Flames reflected in her dark pupils a split second before she slipped back into unconsciousness.

Cash holstered his weapon. She'd taken a nasty hit to the head and then some. She needed medical attention. Now. He slid his hands beneath her thin frame, only then noting that she'd run to the front yard in nothing but a T-shirt and lounge shorts, and hauled her into his chest. *"Aus."*

Bear followed close on his heels like the good companion she'd been trained to be for the Drug Enforcement Agency. With more cartels like *Sangre por Sangre* popping up between the states and butting up against the Mexican border, deploying K9s like her had become standard protocol, but Bear had taken one too many concussions during her service for the agency. Always the first to respond. Always the last one to leave. She'd dedicated her life to saving lives, and in return, he'd saved her when she'd faced being put down. They had an understanding. A partnership. She was part of the team, and he wasn't ever going to leave her behind.

Cash jogged the way he'd come and wrenched the back door of his SUV open. Bear waited for her turn as he laid the woman in his arms across the seat, then took position in the front. He hauled himself behind the steering wheel and flipped around as fast as he dared. Alpine Valley didn't have its own hospital, and the small clinic meant to handle non-life-threatening injuries would be overrun.

Her groan practically vibrated through him from

the backseat and deep into bone. "Son of a bitch… lied."

"That seems uncalled for." Cash barely managed to dodge a police cruiser tearing down the street with its lights and sirens on high alert. His mind raced to fill in the blanks that came with her words. She wasn't conscious. Whatever she'd been through tonight had taken hold and wouldn't let go. It was a defense mechanism. One part of her brain was trying to process the trauma, while the other tried to force her into action. "I'm going to get you help. Okay?"

She didn't answer. Out cold.

Putting her in his sights with the rearview mirror, he couldn't help but catch a glimpse of the devastation behind. It'd take all night for Fire and Rescue to get the flames under control. Cash hit the first number on his speed dial on the phone mounted to the dash. The line only rang once.

"What the hell happened, Meyers?" Jocelyn Carville, Socorro's logistics officer, didn't give him the chance to answer. "Because from where I'm at on the top floor, it looks like an entire town has caught fire."

"You're not wrong." Cash floored the accelerator with another check in the rearview mirror. His backseat companion hadn't moved. "I need additional fire and ambulance units in response from Canon and Ponderosa sent to Alpine Valley. What they have isn't enough. I counted at least three homes on fire and two dozen residents injured. I'm bringing another in."

"Wait. You're bringing who in?" Jocelyn's voice hitched a bit higher.

"Doesn't matter. Can you get me the rigs or not?" he asked.

"I can have them there within thirty minutes." He could practically hear the logistics officer jabbing her finger into the phone. "You owe me."

"I'll have a box of Junior Mints on your desk by morning." Ending the call, he glanced at Bear staring at him from her position in the front seat. "What? I couldn't just leave her there. The clinic is going to be overrun. We have a perfectly good suite at headquarters. The doc will know how to help." She didn't look too convinced. "Don't give me that look. You would've done the same thing. Protocols be damned."

She cut her attention out the passenger side window. Her side of the conversation was over.

Cash carved through town. The blaze overtaking Alpine Valley had spread and gave off a glow seen for miles. Every cell in his body urged him to turn around—to do what he could to help—but he had to trust the police knew what they were doing. He turned the SUV onto a one-way dirt road that led up the mountain that overlooked the valley, pinched between two plateaus.

Socorro Security had become the Pentagon's latest instrument in undermining and disbanding *Sangre por Sangre*. Their operation was smaller than most defense companies, but the private military contractors assembled under its banner were the best the United States military had to offer. Forward observers, logistics, combat control, terrorism, homicide—they did it all, and they did it for people like the woman in his back seat. To protect them against the crushing waves of cartels killing and competing for control.

The corner of the massive compound stood out from the dirt-colored mountains surrounding it. Modern, with sleek corners, bulletproof floor-to-ceiling windows, a flat roof that housed their own chopper pad and a black design that had been carved into the side of the range. The one-million square foot headquarters housed seven operatives in their own rooms, a fleet of SUVs, a chef's kitchen, an oversize gym, an underground garage, a backup generator, an armory and the best security available on the market. This place had become home after his discharge from the marine corp. A place to land after not knowing what to do next—but it was the medical suite Cash needed now.

He dipped the head of the SUV down in the garage with a click of an overhead button and pulled up in front of the elevator doors. He hit the asphalt, Bear jumping free behind him, and rounded to the back seat.

Cash tried not to jar her head more than necessary, hugging her against him. She was still unresponsive, but her delirious name-calling earlier was a good sign she'd pull through. She wasn't talking anymore though, and a sense of urgency simmered in his gut. He wasn't a doctor. While he'd taken a few hits to the head throughout his service, he didn't know anything more than the instinct to get her to a real doctor. He nodded to the elevator door's keypad. *"Tür."*

Bear pressed her front paw to the scanner, and the doors parted.

Once they were inside, a wall of cool air closed in around them as the doors secured into place. His grip automatically tightened on the woman in his arms as the elevator car shot upward. The swelling had reached its peak, but even underneath the bruising and blood, he had a proper glimpse of arched eyebrows, thick eyelashes and a perfect Cupid's bow along her upper lip. He guessed her age somewhere between third-two and thirty-six. No hint of silver or gray in a black mane that must've reached her low back. Fit. Someone who took care of herself. Her breathing was even, deep and accentuated her collarbone across her shoulders. She was beautiful to say the least, but that hadn't stopped the cartel from hurting her.

Bear cocked her head at him, as though sensing he'd taken his eyes off the target. Hell. He hadn't brought her back to headquarters for his own viewing party. She needed immediate help she wasn't going to get back in town.

The elevator pinged, and a world of black expanded before him. The floors, the ceilings, the walls, the art.

Monochrome and practical. Cash picked up his pace. He shoved through the door at the end of the hall, swung the woman onto the bed in the middle of the room and got the attention of Socorro's only doctor, seated behind the desk at the far end.

"Hey, Doc." Pointing to Socorro's only visitor, he tried to contain the battle-ready tension in his voice. "I brought you something."

Don't miss
K-9 Security *by Nichole Severn,*
available January 2024 wherever
Harlequin Intrigue books and ebooks are sold.

www.Harlequin.com

COMING NEXT MONTH FROM

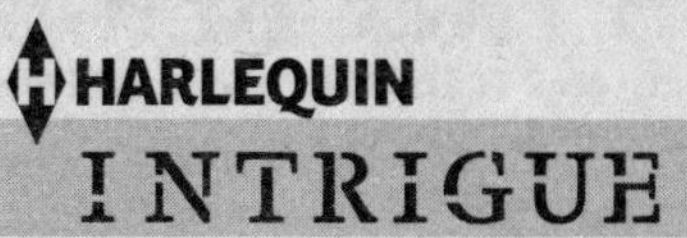

#2199 A PLACE TO HIDE

Lookout Mountain Mysteries • by Debra Webb

Two and a half years ago, Grace Myers, infant son in tow, escaped a serial killer. Now, she'll have to trust Deputy Robert Vaughn to safeguard their identities and lives. The culprit is still on the loose and determined to get even...

#2200 WETLANDS INVESTIGATION

The Swamp Slayings • by Carla Cassidy

Investigator Nick Cain is in the small town of Black Bayou for one reason—to catch a serial killer. But between his unwanted attraction to his partner Officer Sarah Beauregard and all the deadly town secrets he uncovers, will his plan to catch the killer implode?

#2201 K-9 DETECTION

New Mexico Guard Dogs • by Nichole Severn

Jocelyn Carville knows a dangerous cartel is responsible for the Alpine Valley PD station bombing. But convincing Captain Baker Halsey is harder than uncovering the cartel's motive. Until the syndicate's next attack makes their risky partnership inevitable...

#2202 SWIFTWATER ENEMIES

Big Sky Search and Rescue • by Danica Winters

When Aspen Stevens and Detective Leo West meet at a crime scene, they instantly dislike each other. But uncovering the truth about their victim means combining search and rescue expertise and acknowledging the fine line between love and hate even as they risk their lives...

#2203 THE PERFECT WITNESS

Secure One • by Katie Mettner

Security expert Cal Newfellow knows safety is an illusion. But when he's tasked with protecting Marlise, a prosecutor's star witness against an infamous trafficker and murderer, he'll do everything in his power to keep the danger—and his heart—away from her.

#2204 MURDER IN THE BLUE RIDGE MOUNTAINS

The Lynleys of Law Enforcement • by R. Barri Flowers

After a body is discovered in the mountains, special agent Garrett Sneed returns home to work the case with his ex, law enforcement ranger Madison Lynley. Before long, their attraction is heating up...until another homicide reveals a possible link to his mother's unsolved murder. And then the killer sets his sights on Madison...